THE FINDING OF EDEN

DAWN KNOX

British Library Cataloguing in Publication Data A Record of this Publication is available from the British Library

ISBN: 9798832880396

Formatting and Cover © Paul Burridge at www.publishingbuddy.co.uk
Editing – Wendy Ogilvie Editorial Services

To my mum, Amelia May, after whom I named the ship, the Lady Amelia. And to my dad.

Thank you both for believing in me.

CHAPTER ONE

Luck had been with the Bonner family on that sweltering June evening in 1782.

The sun which had blazed mercilessly all day had finally set and the citizens who lived in Black Swan Lane in the City of Westminster were preparing for another humid night filled with the stench of the sewers and the slaughterhouse behind St Margaret's Church.

Halfway along Black Swan Lane in *Peter Allen,* the mercer's shop, Mrs Allen was making her way down the stairs carrying several rolls of velvet with boxes of assorted threads balanced on top. She suddenly realised she'd forgotten the blue silk Mrs Arthur had ordered and swore loudly at the thought of climbing the stairs again. At the same moment, the cat darted past her in pursuit of a rat, sending her tumbling down the remaining steps – the box of threads, the rolls of fabric and most crucially, the candle – falling with her.

Mrs Allen struck her head and during the few minutes she was unconscious, the velvet brushed against the candle. It flared up, setting a length of cotton fabric alight. With astonishing rapidity, the flames leapt onto the countertop and capered left and right, consuming everything in their path. Before passers-by had a chance to spot the blaze or the smoke billowing out of the mercer's windows, the shop had become an inferno.

An evening breeze sprang up which fanned the flames, nudging them towards the perfumer's next door to devour the spirits in the storeroom with a mighty whoosh and to shatter the tiny glass bottles with much cracking and tinkling, and then once they'd done their worst, they danced onwards to the portmanteau seller's next door.

The Bonner family, still in their nightclothes, rushed into the street having been roused by neighbours. With horror, they watched the blaze in the portmanteau seller's shop, their gazes swinging anxiously back and forth across the six shops which separated the fire from *J. Bonner and G. Youngson – Watchmakers.*

The family group was engulfed by people who shuffled right and left, craning their necks to watch the swift progress of the blaze. Nearby, the perfumer and his wife and children were comforted by neighbours who were keeping a wary eye on their own properties. Everyone knew the capricious nature of flames. They were capable of changing direction and reaching across from an overhanging storey on one side of the lane to its counterpart on the other – especially in those stretches of the lane where the gables almost touched. A spark could become an inferno in minutes and no shop was safe. Indeed, entire streets could succumb to a single spark.

The owners of the shops that were next in line to catch fire, joined the uniformed men of the insurance company's fire brigade. Thankfully, most of the shop owners had the identifying iron mark of the Westminster Assurance Company fixed high on their walls. That entitled them to the services of the company's fire brigade, whose men arrived with the hand-drawn fire engine. While some feverishly manned the pump, others held the hose, directing the stream of water onto the flames.

Not everyone in the crowd had a personal interest in the outcome – many had been attracted by the smoke and glow of the flames and had deviated from their evening's plans to gape at the spectacle. However, as the summer night air filled with choking smoke and ash, many resumed their journey and left the unfortunate residents of Black Swan Lane to deal with the damage and loss. After all, fires were a common occurrence in London with its many wooden houses and although this blaze showed promise, there'd certainly been more spectacular infernos.

Joseph Bonner tightly clasped his wife Mary to him, patted the heads of his two daughters and with a brief nod, turned to assist those who'd formed a human chain to convey buckets of water to douse the flames.

Mary grabbed his arm. "Joseph?" she said although she doubted he'd heard her above the wailing of the crowd and the roar of the fire. But she knew him well enough to know he'd understand her concern for him, for their home, for the business he'd inherited from his father and for the unborn child who, God willing, would soon arrive. Joseph's smile and nod told her he'd understood his wife's unspoken appeal to make all well again but above all, to take care. Then he turned and was lost from sight, followed by his apprentice, Jacob.

Mary offered up a prayer to keep her husband and their business safe, because without them both, how would she feed two daughters and the child that was on its way? She wrapped her arms protectively around her swollen belly.

"Look, that one's on fire now," the old woman next to Mary, remarked with satisfaction, spitting crumbs as she spoke. Taking another bite of pie, she pointed out the glow at the top of the apothecary next to the portmanteau business.

"I'll wager there's plenty to burn in there." The old woman cackled gleefully.

Before Mary could reply or at least drag the children away from the crone's obvious delight in others' misery, the uniformed men began to haul the fire pump towards them, now training the spout of water onto the apothecary in an attempt to halt the fire. The crowd moved back to give them space, pushing Mary and her family along the street, away from *J. Bonner and G. Youngson – Watchmakers.* She seized nine-year-old Eva by the hand, for a second, she lost her grip on five-year-old Keziah. Mary screamed her daughter's name as the crush of bodies bore down on them and, with relief, heard her servant, Sarah. "I've got her mistress! I've got her!"

The wind veered slightly, blowing thick, oily smoke down on the crowd and as Mary and Eva began to choke, she dragged the young girl out of the throng, shouting for Sarah to follow with Keziah. She almost wept with relief when she caught sight of her servant with Keziah in her arms, holding the tiny girl's face into her shoulder to protect her from the smoke.

"Where will we go, mistress?" Sarah's eyes bulged with fear.

Mary hesitated. She needed to get them all away from the noxious air, yet she wanted to make sure Joseph and Jacob were safe.

And then nature took a hand. Mary's waters broke and she knew she had no choice.

"We'll go to my sister's," she shouted and doubled over as pain shot through her belly.

"Mama! Mama!" The flames reflected in Eva's enormous, dark eyes as she threw her arms around her mother and clung to her.

Sarah handed Keziah to Eva. Shepherding the girls before her, she elbowed people aside with her strong arms and helped Mary towards the corner of the street where the crowds were thinner. As they turned into St Margaret's Street, she took Keziah from Eva and perched the tiny girl on her hip. Then, with a protective arm around Mary, she led the way towards Calico Alley, where Mary's sister, Hester, lived with her husband when he was home from the sea.

"Hold on tight, Eva, there's a good lass," Sarah said, and the young girl gripped the servant's apron.

They'd barely walked a few paces before there was a tremendous crash followed by screams and wailing from Black Swan Lane.

Mary groaned and stopped, wanting to turn back but another wave of pain coursed through her.

"Come away, mistress, there's nowt we can do and you need help."

With a sob Mary allowed herself to be led towards Hester's house, holding her arms protectively around the unborn child.

Finally, they were on the doorstep of the Dudley's shabby cottage and Sarah thumped her large, ham-like fist against the weathered door. When nobody came, she continued to hammer frantically. Mary began to fear her sister wasn't home although it was difficult to imagine where she might be since they had no other family in London and Hester had few friends.

A nervous voice called from above. "Be off with you!"

Sarah stepped back hoping to be seen in the darkness of the alley and shouted out who she was and that her mistress needed help.

"Mary?" the woman at the upstairs window called, less fearful now.

"Hester! Please, let us in!" Mary gasped as more pain shot through her.

The window closed and there was a slight delay while Hester lit a candle and padded downstairs to unlock the door. She stood aside to allow her uninvited guests to enter the untidy, dingy cottage but Sarah hung back, ensuring the two girls and her mistress were safely inside. Mary turned to her but before she could say anything, another spasm seized her and she cried out.

"Yes, mistress," Sarah said, having guessed Mary's unspoken thoughts, "First I'll send the midwife, then I'll find the master." And with that, she strode back along Calico Alley, her petticoats swishing.

Mrs Haywood, the midwife, arrived shortly after and peeled off her dripping cloak. "'Tis rainin' fit for an ark, so it is! Now, how can I be of assistance?" She wiped her face on her apron before following Hester upstairs.

"Not long now, mistress," she said to Mary after examining her. But Mary's eyes were on the door, waiting for Sarah's return with news of her husband. Surely the rain would quench the flames? And if it did, would it be too late for the watchmaker's shop?

Finally, there was a knock on the cottage door and Mary recognised Sarah's footsteps stomping up the stairs.

"Master and Jacob are well, the fire is out and the shop safe," Sarah said with a smile and Mary sank back onto the pillow in relief. Praise the Lord her family were no longer in danger. Now she needed her strength to bring the newest member safely into the world.

Henry Joseph Bonner was born in the early hours of 10 June 1782 – the day following the fire in which seven buildings had burnt to the ground and also the night of the great storm which had taken London by surprise and flooded areas around the Fleet River, drowning two men.

The blaze had finally been halted at about the same time as Master

Bonner had slipped into the midwife's hands although, for some time, the fire appeared to be uncontrollable with strong winds accelerating the spread of the flames along Black Swan Lane.

It was only the decision to knock down the empty bookshop that had helped change the outcome and since, previously, many had predicted the derelict building would fall on its own, the demolition hadn't taken much effort. The firemen's quick thinking and speedy actions in creating a firebreak meant Joseph's watchmaker's shop was also spared.

There was now a gaping hole in the street where the blackened, burnt-out shops and the ramshackle booksellers had once been, although it was unlikely that on its own, the destruction of the building would have been sufficient to stop the flames leaping across. Indeed, the fire was reaching such a frenzy, it might easily have spanned the gap – but for the summer storm. The torrential downpour had drenched the firemen and helpers while aiding them in dampening the inferno, and the cloudburst had obligingly continued until the fire was brought under control.

It was early morning before everyone was satisfied the embers had been completely extinguished and Joseph and his apprentice wearily trudged through the sodden streets to his sister-in-law's house where he met his son for the first time.

After an hour's sleep and a meal of stale bread, cheese and ale – all Hester's servant had to offer him, Joseph kissed his wife, his two sleeping daughters and his son's downy head, then roused Jacob and went back to Black Swan Lane. The dawn light shone grey on the blackened ruins and revealed how close his watchmaker's shop had been to devastation. Inside the shop, the odour of burnt wood and smoke lingered strongly and he and Jacob climbed the stairs to his workshop on the first floor and set about cleaning the ash and soot off the workbench and all the precious tools.

A shocked George Youngson, Joseph's business partner, arrived several hours later. He explained he'd been at a cockfight at the Royal Cockpit, near St James's Park, the previous evening and hadn't heard about the fire until one of his servants had mentioned it on his arrival home in the early hours. Joseph knew it would have made no difference if George had been there the previous night because he was not a man who dirtied his hands and he'd undoubtedly have merely watched. He was, by his own admission, a partner in the business solely for the profit which during the last few years had been good due to Joseph's skill and hard work.

Years before, Joseph's father and Mr Youngson Snr had established the business with Mr Youngson being a silent partner, and when both men had died, they'd passed their shares in the business on to their sons. Like his father, George Jr had no interest in watchmaking which suited Joseph well because the day-to-day running of the business was left to him and George merely took his cut of the profits.

Now, George's gaze darted about, checking the half-finished pieces that Joseph and the apprentice were working on.

"But we'll be able to fulfil our orders?" He ran his finger along the workbench and examined the black residue on his fingertip with disdain. "It appears Fortune was with you, old fellow." He wiped the grime away with his handkerchief. "And just as well because I lost heavily last night. I placed a hundred guineas on a cock which... well, let's just say he was a great disappointment, so I can well do without unnecessary expense at the moment." He frowned at the smudge on the snowy handkerchief made by the soot on his fingertip. "And you're certain nothing was damaged?"

"No, nothing, and once everything is clean, it'll be business as usual." Joseph had previously noted George was happy to take the profit but not so pleased to pay for breakages or new equipment or tools.

George nodded, obviously satisfied the premises were undamaged and the business was still viable – yet he'd not enquired how Mrs Bonner or Joseph's daughters were.

"Good, good, then I shall delay you no more." George checked his watch. "I have a busy day ahead, so I'll bid you good morning." And with that, taking care not to brush against anything, he left the workshop.

Sarah arrived shortly after, accompanied by Polly, Hester's servant, and the two women began work, cleaning the family's living quarters on the third floor. Sarah reported that Mary and the baby were doing well, although, she said, "The mistress is uncommon tired this morning and will remain abed. The shock of the fire, I reckon."

Neighbours called in the shop during the morning, some to enquire if Joseph needed help and others simply to gape at the blackened ruins. Many expressed their amazement at the Bonner family's good luck. Despite the arduous work of cleaning, tears welled up behind Joseph's eyelids as he wholeheartedly agreed with them.

How could he have known that would be the last bit of good luck his family would enjoy?

CHAPTER TWO

Within a few days, Joseph and his family had moved back into their home in Black Swan Lane. Henry Joseph Bonner roared loudly when placed in the cot that had belonged to his sisters before him. But he soon became accustomed to the rhythm, sounds and smells of his new home. Sarah singing as she worked in the kitchen. The tip, tip, tip of tiny hammers on metal ringing out in the workshop. His elder sisters squealing with delight when he grabbed their proffered fingers and he recognised his mother's laboured breathing as she tried to regain her strength. Eventually, Mary became so weak that Joseph called the physician who bled her and announced her heart was struggling. But despite the bed rest he prescribed, Mary grew weaker and at the end of July, she died.

"Where's Mama?" Keziah asked, her bottom lip quivering and tears brimming on her lower eyelids.

Eva put her arm around her. Keziah had seen the coffin lowered into the grave in St Margaret's churchyard, but her five-year-old mind hadn't been able to grasp that her mother, who she'd kissed while she lay in the coffin earlier, was still in the box on which earth was now being tossed. Eva shivered. She couldn't believe it either.

Papa took the girls' hands and silently led them away from the graveside followed by a snivelling Sarah, dabbing her eyes and holding a gurgling Henry who would not remember the funeral of the woman who'd given him life but whom he'd only known for a few weeks.

The loss of their mother had been bad enough but a month later, when Sarah received a letter which she brought to Joseph to read to her, it became clear the family were about to suffer another loss.

A look of sadness and resignation came over his face as he read, then sighing deeply, he suggested Sarah sit down. Her mother had died and she'd been called back to Norfolk to look after her brothers and sisters. Sarah was torn, having been away from her own home for several years and now feeling closer to Joseph and his children than the brood she hadn't seen since she'd come to London four years ago, aged sixteen.

"Don't leave us!" Eva flung her arms around Sarah when she realised she'd be going back to Norfolk.

"Hush, child," Joseph said, "you of all people should understand the pain of losing a mother. Don't make this harder for Sarah."

Eva clamped her lips together and was silent then, but she didn't agree with Papa. Sarah was grown up and adults didn't need their mothers – not like she, Kezzie and Henry did. Sarah hadn't seen her mother for years. And now Mama had gone, they all relied on kind, gentle Sarah.

The farewell had been tearful with the girls clinging to Sarah's skirts, begging her to stay. Henry, still only a few months old, didn't realise the second woman who'd loved him during his short time on earth was being torn from his life.

Finally, Joseph prised the two girls from Sarah and nodded sadly for her to leave although there were tears in his grey eyes. His heart was like a cold stone in his chest. Sarah had served his family well and having shown great affection for his beloved late wife – she'd become part of the family, not simply a servant.

Joseph replaced her with an older, rather serious widow, whose children were already grown. Betsy was methodical and conscientious but she had little time for Eva, Keziah or Henry. Having brought up children of her own, she limited her affection to her own grandchildren.

With the benefit of eight years of her mother's love and with those still fresh in her mind, Eva assumed the role of mother to Keziah and Henry.

Joseph was grateful his eldest daughter was taking responsibility for the other two children – he had unwelcome distractions of his own when he realised his partner, George, had borrowed a large sum of money to pay his gambling debts. Joseph challenged him about the missing money, he denied it, but finally confessed and swore he'd pay it back. Joseph knew he'd have to work harder to keep the business afloat – and keep a closer eye on the accounts.

It was Betsy who inadvertently revealed the next disaster that would befall the Bonner household.

Eva was minding three-year-old Henry – an energetic and inquisitive child who could often be found using clothes pegs or spoons, imitating his father with his watchmaking tools – while Betsy sorted the laundry, grumbling and complaining about the bloodstains on master's handkerchiefs. At first, Eva thought Papa must have cut himself on one of his tools which was unusual because Joseph was very careful and nimble-fingered. It was only when the family next ate a meal together she noticed her father cough into his handkerchief and a brief flash of red before he screwed it up in the palm of his hand and tucked it back into his pocket. She looked at him questioningly but he averted his gaze.

Mr Pinder, the schoolmaster, had coughed up blood, Eva

8

remembered, and he'd died of consumption the previous year. But surely, Papa didn't have the same condition? It was inconceivable he should be taken from them too. The mutton she was chewing seemed as dry as sawdust but she dared not spit it out for fear of drawing Betsy's indignation and questions, and with much effort, she finally managed to swallow it.

By the beginning of 1787, Joseph had deteriorated so much he relied heavily on Jacob who'd served his apprenticeship and was now a journeyman working in the business along with a new apprentice. Joseph still managed the accounts although periodically, George Youngson came by, supposedly to help with the books but by December, it was obvious Joseph was seriously ill. On Christmas Eve 1787, there was a large fall of snow and it was impossible to keep out the chilly draughts that blew the bed hangings on Joseph's bed, but the family who gathered around as he fought for breath, scarcely noticed. The chill in each heart was icier than the weather.

On the day of the burial, a bitter wind blew the powdery snow into flurries, freezing the large group of mourners who'd gathered shivering around the graveside next to where Mary Bonner lay in Saint Margaret's churchyard. By the time they returned to Black Swan Lane, snow covered nearly everything except the shop doorstep which was almost clear, as if there'd been many people going in and out. But the shop had been closed because everyone had been at the burial and the snow that had fallen after the family had left, would have covered the footsteps they'd made earlier.

When Jacob opened the door, the reason for so much activity into and out of the premises soon became obvious. The shop had been stripped of all its stock. For several shocked seconds, everyone looked around unable to believe the bare shelves, then Jacob elbowed past Eva and took the stairs two at a time up to the workshop on the first floor. His cry of anguish and the thumping of his fist against the workbench brought the others running to see what had happened. The workshop too, was bare, the watchmaking tools and parts had gone.

Jacob rushed out into the cold to alert the parish constable but by the time anyone visited George Youngson's lodgings, it was too late – he'd packed everything and had gone.

"'E were in a mighty rush to leave," his landlady told the constable and his men, "I 'eard one of his manservants say something about a ship, so it's my guess he's left the country."

Several neighbours reported Mr Youngson and several servants had been in and out of the shop all morning but no one had challenged him because they all knew he was Joseph's partner.

Further investigation showed George had cleared the business bank account with some papers signed by Joseph, presumably when was too ill to spot any of George's underhand tricks.

Eva had no more tears left to cry. The only money left was that which Joseph had intended to deposit in the bank but had forgotten to give to George. The following day, Jacob mumbled his apologies and regretfully handed in his notice. He had to find employment quickly and hope he'd be accepted without any tools until he could afford to replace them. The apprentice found another master where he could finish his apprenticeship. Betsy alone remained to look after Eva, Keziah and Henry.

By March, Betsy and Eva counted the money remaining, and it was obvious, once the rent had been paid, there would be very little left.

"It's time your Aunt Hester did her bit for the family," Betsy said. "I'd have thought she'd have been around to check on her nieces and nephew afore this. But we haven't seen a suspicion of her. There's nothing for it, lass," she said to Eva, "you're going to have to ask for her help. We'll go tomorrow. Leave the talking to me."

Eva accompanied Betsy to Calico Alley and on the way wondered if it wouldn't have been wiser to go alone. Betsy could be blunt, and Eva anticipated this was likely to be one of those times – if the determined stride and set line of her jaw was anything to go by. She'd seen Betsy tackle many a stubborn shopkeeper over a purchase which she considered shoddy or substandard and her tongue proved to be sharper and her determination greater than any of them. Eva knew her lack of tact gained her few friends, and although Betsy always won the battle, ultimately, she lost the war because she never received good service again. But perhaps that was behaviour she reserved for tradesmen and she'd be more polite with her former employer's family.

It proved not to be so. Aunt Hester took her time opening the door, her face pinched and her thin hair in disarray, as if she'd only just risen from bed despite it being almost noon. She was first shocked, then annoyed and finally outraged at Betsy's forthright accusation of neglect of her nieces and nephew, and her demand to take them into her home.

"There's scarcely room for my husband and myself when he returns from the sea," Aunt Hester said spiritedly although she stepped back slightly when Betsy leaned forward.

"I'm sure you have room for three young children." Betsy poked the air between them with her finger. "No need to take me in, I intend to stay with my daughter."

That was the first Eva knew about Betsy leaving them and her heart lurched even though the servant hadn't been the mother she, Keziah and Henry had needed. Or perhaps Betsy, having seen Aunt Hester's house for the first time, decided it was too small. More likely, knowing Betsy, she'd taken a dislike to the other woman and simply wanted nothing to do with her.

Aunt Hester had always been remote, never having visited Black Swan Lane and now, angry red spots flared on her cheeks and her eyes glittered with fury. Nevertheless, she agreed to take the children in.

At the beginning of April, what was left of the Bonner family, arrived in Calico Alley with their belongings, assisted by Betsy. Aunt Hester bristled at Betsy's parting advice to act like an aunt and take care of her nieces and nephew, and she slammed the front door before Betsy had a chance to say goodbye to the children.

Several weeks after their arrival, Aunt Hester's maid packed her bag and left. Eva was unsure whether it was because of their presence in the cramped cottage or because Aunt Hester had dismissed her because she assumed her nieces would work for their keep. After that, Eva and Keziah ran the household while her aunt rose later and later and occasionally, remained in bed all day.

Aunt Hester often complained of headaches and Eva knew she had a small bottle of medicine on her bedside table, a few drops of which she regularly added to her gin. Shortly after she'd taken them, Aunt Hester could be heard snoring and muttering in her sleep. The first time Eva realised how deeply the medicine affected her aunt, she'd tried to wake her when the landlord had called and finding Aunt Hester limp and unresponsive, she'd believed she was dying. The landlord, however, obviously recognised the bottle on the table and after dipping his finger in the almost empty glass of gin and sucking it, he winced. "Laudanum," he said with an irritable sniff. He added he'd return on the morrow and that Eva should tell Mrs Dudley to expect him at the same time of day. Aunt Hester had been ready the following day to pay the landlord although she then complained of a headache and went back to bed.

Late one afternoon, a stout woman knocked at the door asking for Aunt Hester. Although subdued, she came downstairs and a whispered conversation took place on the doorstep.

When the woman left, Aunt Hester looked at Eva with wide, horror-stricken eyes.

"What is it, Aunt? Is it bad news?"

"Your uncle's ship has docked." Aunt Hester clasped her hands together and held them to her chest.

"Isn't that good news?" Eva asked with a puzzled frown. Aunt Hester never mentioned her husband so it hadn't occurred to Eva she wouldn't be pleased to see him.

"Best you children be out when he returns." Aunt Hester wrung her hands. "Best I talk to him first and explain."

"Is he on his way?" Eva was alarmed at her aunt's anxiety.

"It's unlikely," said Aunt Hester. "He'll stop at the tavern first. So best you three go out for a while."

"Out? But where?"

"I don't know!" Aunt Hester snapped.

"But how long should we stay out?"

"It depends how well the voyage went and how sober he is when he gets home."

"Where will we go until then?" Panic crept into Eva's voice.

Aunt Hester's jaw clenched angrily and she moved towards a chipped, china vase which she turned upside down and tipped the contents onto her palm. She sifted through and picked out several coins, holding them out to Eva.

"There are plenty of food sellers along the Strand. Don't spend it all. I expect some change when you get back. And watch out for the pickpockets. Now go!" Aunt Hester glanced nervously at the door and nibbled her lower lip. "I need time to speak to your uncle."

Aware of the tension, Henry started to cry.

"Perhaps go to St Margaret's," Aunt Hester suggested in slightly kinder tones, as they were putting on their cloaks. She opened the door for them to speed them out and then closed it as soon as they were in the alley.

"Do we have to go to church? I don't like Mr Peters, he stares at me from the pulpit. He's got horrid eyes. And he spits when he's preaching. I'm hungry. Can't we go and find something to eat?" Keziah asked.

"Will we be back after bedtime?" Henry tugged Eva's sleeve hopefully.

Despite the shock of having been turned out by her aunt, Eva realised she was looking forward to wandering in London during the evening – something her father had always forbidden. The safest place would be the church although the thought of sitting in draughty St Margaret's with the possibility of encountering the forbidding rector with the accusing stare was not appealing.

"We don't have to go to church, do we?" Keziah asked again.

"No, Kezzie, let's go to the Strand and buy something to eat." On several occasions, Eva had accompanied Papa along the Strand when he'd delivered watches to the grand houses of wealthy clients and it had seemed so grand. She knew the area around Black Swan Lane well – the way to the school, the way to the market and to the shops Mama, Sarah and Betsy had frequented – but she knew very little about the surrounding alleys, courts and streets. Now was the time to learn. She was fourteen and she ought to know her way around her home town.

Too late Eva realised she had no way of knowing when it would be safe to return to Aunt Hester's house without knocking at the door and risking her aunt's anger.

Holding Henry and Keziah's hands, Eva walked quickly towards St Margaret's Street. The upper storeys of the tumbledown buildings on either side of Calico Alley reached towards each other blocking out the light, leaving the litter-strewn passage in semi-darkness – even during the brightest day. It was not a place to linger. But once on wider, busier St Margaret's Street, Eva felt safer although she was surprised to see so many people out walking, many dressed in elaborate evening attire.

The Thames lay to her right; the Strand in the opposite direction and most people were heading that way.

"Is it time for St Bartholomew's Fair?" Keziah's eyes were wide with hope.

"No, Kezzie, that's in August." But Eva could see why her sister was confused. There was a festive atmosphere such as there'd been on the occasions when Papa had taken them to the fair near St Bartholomew's Hospital. Eva considered; had the day-to-day drudgery of life at Aunt Hester's dulled her to life outside? Surely it couldn't be like this every evening? But she couldn't think of a feast day nor a fair which would be taking place now.

"Can we see bear-baiting?" Henry skipped along, caught up in the lively atmosphere. "Betsy told me about it. She said it was exciting."

"It's cruel!" Keziah said, "I wouldn't like to see it at all! I don't know how you can be so unkind Henry!"

"It's not unkind at all, Kezzie, it's like cockfighting. It's something gentlemen watch."

"Gentlemen!" Keziah scoffed. "Papa never watched animals fight!" She tossed her dark curls. "Did he, Evie?"

"No," Eva said thoughtfully. She realised with shock, how ignorant she was of what was going on around her. Since she'd been at her aunt's, she hadn't read a newspaper, unless it was one she'd glanced at that had been discarded in the street. And with Betsy gone, the only time Eva learned what was happening in the world was when a shopkeeper had time to gossip or when she overheard someone's conversation while queuing in a shop.

Until her father had become ill, he'd kept abreast of the latest news and had discussed anything topical with his family at dinner although Eva had known from Betsy that more was going on than was discussed at their table. But now, she scarcely knew what day it was – much less whether it was a feast day.

There was so much she didn't know.

Papa had been strict about them not going out at night and although pupils at school had told her about diverting things taking place, Eva thought they were rare occurrences. Her father had taken them to watch the Lord Mayor's Procession with its colourful City Companies' ceremonial barges on the river, the May Fair and, of course, the renowned St Bartholomew's Fair with its swing boats and roundabouts, and wonderful acrobats and rope-dancers. But although Papa had let them see the puppets and dancing and even go on the roundabout, he hadn't allowed them to watch anything he thought unsuitable such as the stalls with strange monsters and misshapen men and women. He'd urged them on, not permitting them to stop and 'gawp', as he'd put it.

Papa had wanted their safety but had he over-protected them?

"Mistress Bonner!" A shout came from the other side of the street, outside the Brown Cow Tavern where a young man had raised his hand and was waving. He now came across the road towards them, picking his way through the filth and stepping over the gutter running down the middle of the road. Four young men called good-naturedly after him telling him they'd be late but he shouted he'd only be a moment.

Eva recognised him instantly. It was Jacob Wild, former apprentice and journeyman who'd worked for her father. She'd always idolised Jacob with his handsome face and quick wit although she'd been very careful to conceal her interest in him, knowing it would provoke teasing within the family, and possibly even her father's anger. There was a seven-year age gap between them which a few years ago had been much greater than it appeared now.

"Look, Evie!" Keziah shouted, waving excitedly, "it's Jacob!"

"Hush!" Eva said sharply aware of how young and unsophisticated she must appear, out strolling with her brother and sister – and she was immediately ashamed of herself for being so abrupt with Keziah.

Eva smiled in what she hoped was a grown-up way at Jacob.

"You can always rely on Jacob to find the prettiest girl!" one of the young men on the other side of the road, shouted, his voice slurred.

"Who'll take a wager on how long it'll take Jacob to bed her?" one of the others yelled and they laughed uproariously as they took on the wager.

"Don't listen to them," Jacob said although he was smiling as if he was pleased with his reputation.

Eva was shocked at the young men's ribald comments and even more so because Jacob was taking such pains to talk to her. She'd been jealous of the girls who'd come into the shop looking for Jacob. Papa had always sent them away. Jacob had been kind to Eva. He'd conducted himself respectfully, in a way one would expect an apprentice and later a journeyman to behave when speaking to the daughter of his master. But she'd always felt so young in his presence.

Ignoring his friends' bawdy comments, Jacob was as polite and deferential as he'd been when he worked for Papa. Eva was disappointed that it appeared the relationship was to carry on at that level. Not, of course, that he'd be interested in her. And yet, something was different between them. There was a gleam in his eyes which had never been there before or perhaps she simply hadn't noticed. No, she decided something had changed between them.

"And where are you off to this evening?" Jacob asked.

"Evie's taking us to the Strand," Keziah said before Eva could answer.

"Indeed!" Jacob tickled her under the chin and made her giggle. "And what would the Bonner family be intending to do there?"

"We were going for a walk," Eva said nonchalantly as if that was something they did every evening.

"If you have no firm plans, you could always come with me."

Eva's heart skipped a beat, not able to believe that he'd invited her to walk out with him. Admittedly the invitation included Keziah and Henry but even so, she could scarcely believe this good fortune.

"Where are you going?" Keziah asked and Eva glanced at her crossly. She didn't care where Jacob was going, she'd have gone anywhere if it meant she could have walked by his side for a while.

"Vauxhall Pleasure Gardens. Mary Sorprendo is singing tonight."

"Will there be food?" Keziah asked.

Jacob laughed. "More food than you can imagine! So, what do you say? Will you come Mistress Keziah?" He tickled her under the chin again.

Eva held her breath. If either her brother or sister refused to go, she'd have to decline.

"Will there be bear-baiting?" Henry looked up at Jacob hopefully.

Jacob laughed. "I doubt it, but there'll be music and dancing."

Henry scowled.

"And sometimes..." Jacob bent towards Henry and in a loud whisper, he added, "there are fistfights." He winked conspiratorially at the boy. "And of course, we'll have supper..."

Henry's eyes lit up. "Can we go, Evie, please?"

Eva pretended to consider and then quickly said in what she hoped was a very grown-up way, "Yes, I believe that would be more diverting than the Strand."

Jacob took Keziah's hand, then held out his arm to Eva and she took it, hoping to hide her blushes as she insisted Henry hold her other hand.

Would Papa have approved? Eva doubted it. At some stage, he'd surely have permitted her to go into society. But she'd never know if he'd consider this too soon. Holding Jacob's arm was perfectly seemly, she told herself, despite the continuing comments from Jacob's friends. This was merely a former employee courteously escorting his previous master's family out for the evening.

Yet while she attempted to convince herself everything was respectable, in her heart she yearned for it to be otherwise and for Keziah and Henry to be home, leaving her out with Jacob alone.

That, however, she accepted as fantasy – and highly unlikely – even if Jacob was making her feel as though they were alone together. He held her arm closely to his side and every so often leaned towards her to whisper in her ear, his breath brushing across her cheek. He pointed out someone he knew or recognised, such as Lord This or Lady That or he covertly drew her attention to an outrageous hat decorated with exotic feathers or yards of lace which some grand lady was wearing. He was creating such an intimate world around them, she was surprised to feel Henry dragging behind and to hear him wail he was tired and to ask peevishly how much longer before they got there.

Eva realised in alarm they'd been walking for some time and she had no idea where they were but with Jacob beside her what did it matter? Nevertheless, Keziah also was beginning to lag and Eva wondered if it was much further. Henry was a far more obliging child than Keziah who was headstrong and uncompromising and would make a fuss if she became weary – regardless of the attention and probable derision of Jacob's friends. Eva glanced anxiously at her sister but she was looking about excitedly at the people milling around them. The crowds appeared to be heading in the same direction and as they rounded a bend in the street, Eva saw the river and heard the cries of watermen touting for fares. With a gasp of dismay, she remembered they'd have to cross the

Thames on a boat to get to Vauxhall Pleasure Gardens. The breath caught in her throat. How could she have been so stupid? Aunt Hester had given her enough to buy a pie each, not for a journey across the river. And then it occurred to her there would also be an entrance fee for the Pleasure Gardens. How foolish she would appear when she told Jacob they couldn't go with him after all. But there was nothing for it. She'd have to confess now before the waterman demanded money.

Eva swallowed and looked up at Jacob about to tell him they wouldn't be able to go with him after all when he turned to her and said, "I hope you'll allow me to pay for you all, this evening, Mistress Bonner. It would give me great pleasure. Your father was a good master. He treated me like one of the family, so this is my way of paying him the respect he deserved."

"Th...thank you. We'd be most grateful..."

Relief flooded through her, immediately followed by disappointment. So, he was fulfilling a duty. Well, of course! It was unlikely he'd choose to be with someone as young and unfashionable. Her clothes were of good quality but they were well-worn and old. They were suitable for shopping but not for an evening out. And even worse, just recently, she'd noticed her bodice was much too tight. If Mama had lived longer, she'd have ensured her daughter had a suitable wardrobe but that had been outside of Papa's experience. And now, Aunt Hester seemed to have very little interest in anyone other than herself.

Gradually, the crush of people eased as the members of Jacob's party found themselves near the bottom of the steps leading down to the river and the watermen, who urged people into their boats. Hugh, the most outspoken of Jacob's friends, stepped forward and agreed a price with a sandy-haired waterman who smiled, showing blackened and missing teeth as he helped them into the boat.

The waterman was a cheery fellow and he welcomed them, although he made it clear he wouldn't allow the young men to indulge in any horseplay. His enormous hands and well-muscled arms were obviously sufficient to persuade Hugh and the others to remain seated which meant they had time during the crossing to tease Jacob, taunting him about his 'new wife and family' and Eva, with cheeks aflame watched the approaching southern bank with longing.

Once out of the boat and up the stairs, Henry who was becoming more and more excited, asked loudly, "Is it far, Evie?"

Her cheeks flamed. She had no idea.

"Not far now, young man," Jacob said, perhaps understanding Eva's predicament, after all he'd lived as part of her family and had seen how she and Keziah had been raised. She clung more tightly to his arm and smiled up at him to show her appreciation. As so many gentlemen and ladies were alighting from the boats and making their way up the steps, they briefly lost Hugh, John, Will and Tom. Eva hoped they wouldn't find them again but by the time they'd reached the street, Jacob's friends were waiting for them.

To Eva's surprise, they headed towards a large house and it wasn't until they were closer she realised that admittance to the Gardens was through a large entrance in the building and again, Jacob had money ready and quietly made it clear he was going to pay for them all. She felt crushed by her naïveté but grateful to Jacob for his sensitivity.

The crowd surged forward but once the various couples and parties were through the bottleneck of the entrance and inside the Gardens, they headed off in different directions. Ahead, Eva could see the Grand Walk, flanked by enormous elm trees along which ladies and gentlemen promenaded.

"Leave it to John and me to arrange supper," Hugh said, but they hadn't gone far when two smartly dressed women approached them and with much fluttering of fans and flirtatious looks, they engaged the men in conversation.

One of the women slipped her arm through Hugh's. The other placed her hand on John's arm as Hugh looked back over his shoulder at the others, winked, and then walked off briskly down the Grand Walk with his female companion.

"Come, Will," Tom said, "let's see if the ladies have any friends. I'll wager they do. Book a supper booth for us, old chap," he said to Jacob. He and Will hurried after Hugh, John and their ladies.

"Are you meeting friends here?" Eva was confused by Tom's comments. The two women had behaved in such a friendly manner to Hugh and John, they must have been sweethearts. Yet Tom seemed to be urging Will to find out if the women had friends. Surely, they would know? But mostly, Eva was dismayed at the thought of women joining them. They would certainly be older and worldlier – and not accompanied by a young girl and an even younger boy. Would Jacob regret having asked them to join him for the evening, and then resent her? But other than a brief, yet irritated glance at his friends who'd now disappeared into the milling throng, Jacob didn't seem annoyed. Indeed, he'd crouched down and pointed out a man with a tiny monkey on his shoulder to a delighted Henry.

When he stood up, there was no suggestion of disappointment or resentment and he offered Eva his arm and led them to a large, open area that he called the Grove. In the middle was an ornate multi-storeyed structure where he said the orchestra would later play and Mrs Sorprendo would sing. Musicians were already in position, tuning their instruments and chattering loudly while many onlookers waited patiently for the performance.

At the far end of the Grove were the supper boxes, each one ornately decorated with murals and coloured lights and containing a table and eight chairs. Eva hadn't realised they'd be sitting down to a proper supper and knew Keziah and Henry would have been happy sharing a pie from a street seller. She wondered anxiously how long it would be before Keziah started complaining about being hungry, and Henry joined in, but thankfully, they were completely absorbed by everything around them, and as soon as Jacob had reserved a box, he once again put his arm out for Eva and suggested they promenade along one of the avenues.

"We must go and see the artificial cascade." He checked his watch. "It starts in twenty minutes, so we've plenty of time to stroll along the Grand Walk."

As they were watching a juggler throw coloured balls in the air, a pretty, young, blonde dressed in a pink silk gown approach Jacob. She smiled at him, ignoring Eva and laid her hand on his arm in an intimate way as if she knew him well. He dropped Eva's arm and stepped towards her.

"Mr Wild, how marvellous to see you again," she said turning her head on one side coquettishly. "Oh, but you have company and I'm obviously intruding. What a shame..." She batted her eyelids. "Another time, perhaps? I believe you know where to find me..." Then with a toss of her head she walked off.

Jacob's cheeks were flushed but he said nothing, and Eva didn't ask who the woman was, after all he hadn't intended for her to join him this evening. His friends were nothing to do with her but it was obvious the blonde woman considered herself closer than a mere acquaintance.

As the juggler finished and bowed to the applause of the audience, Keziah and Henry ran back to Eva, and Jacob crouched down and pretended to produce a shilling from the young boy's ear which he presented with a flourish. Eva protested but Jacob said Henry had found it fair and square and therefore, it belonged to him. Henry fixed her with an anxious look, afraid she'd tell him to give it back. She wanted to insist he return it but she had a feeling the shilling had been used as a distraction to avoid any questions about the blonde woman. A stab of jealousy urged her to allow her brother to keep the shilling – too much for a diversionary trick – a penny would have done as well. So, let him pay, she thought, and told Henry if Jacob wanted him to have it, he could keep it. Jacob smiled up at her and Henry tucked the coin in his pocket quickly, in case she changed her mind. Jacob's flush had faded and it seemed that all awkwardness had been smoothed away. It would be discourteous to bring up the woman again and really, his friends were none of her business.

Taking Eva's arm once more, Jacob steered them left, down a side avenue and joined a large group of people. The crowd was waiting in front of an enormous structure concealed by a screen on which was painted a rustic scene. Jacob checked his pocket watch and picking Henry up, he sat him on his shoulders just as a bell rang loudly and the crowd began to murmur. The screen slowly moved to one side, to reveal what looked and sounded like water running down a cascade.

"Is it real?" Henry gasped.

Jacob laughed. "I believe it's an illusion done with sheets of tin," he whispered to Henry. "They're being moved to look like water. But don't tell the ladies, they think it's real!"

Henry smiled conspiratorially and agreed not to tell.

When they returned to the Grand Walk, hundreds of coloured, globe lights were aglow, lighting up the walks as if the Gardens were a fairy grotto. By the time they arrived at the Grove, Jacob's friends were waiting for them, listening to the musicians who were already playing.

Hugh smiled a slow, self-satisfied smirk. He whispered in Jacob's ear and patted his shoulder as if to console him. Although Eva couldn't hear what Hugh was saying, his gaze caused her to blush.

"Did you book a box?" John asked, "I'm famished."

"Number twenty-four."

At the supper boxes, a waiter took the ticket and showed them to the correct booth where he seated Eva and the children. Hugh ordered cold meats, cheese, salads and bread and butter. "And bring us a quart of your best arrack punch. No. Make that two."

When the food and drink arrived, Jacob poured a small amount of the punch into a glass for Eva. "It's strong, so it's best the little ones don't have any."

How considerate of him. And how marvellous that he'd given her some, although she suppressed a cough when she sipped hers.

"What is it?" she asked once she was sure she could speak without choking.

"Arrack, rum and sugar." He held his glass up to examine the amber liquid. "Vauxhall Gardens is well-known for its arrack punch." He drank a large mouthful and passed Eva a plate of cold meats. "It's also renowned for its ham," he said, slipping a fork beneath a slice and holding it up. "People say it's cut so thinly, you can read a newspaper through it."

When most of the food had gone, Hugh called for tarts, custards and brandy. The conversation had been lively during the meal and as the young men drank heavily, their whispered conversations became louder – loud enough for Eva to hear a few shocking fragments of conversation relating to the men's earlier disappearance with the two young women. How could she have been so stupid? She knew all about whores operating in London and she often saw them when she was out shopping but she'd never seen such well-dressed women plying their trade. Betsy had been the first to point out to her the bedraggled, dirty women who were so desperate for custom, they were quite blatant about what was on offer. She'd had to explain exactly what was on offer and Eva had been shocked. Since neither Mama nor Papa had ever referred to such a thing, she wondered if Betsy had made it up. However, once her eyes had been opened, many things she hadn't understood before began to make sense.

The women who'd accompanied Hugh and his friends were young, fresh and beautiful – nothing like the desperate women Eva had seen in Covent Garden. And now she realised the blonde girl who'd approached Jacob was a whore, and for a second, she was appalled. Reverend Peters, with his intense stare, had condemned such women from the pulpit and her father had also described them as shameless creatures, yet here in this lively company the fact that four young men had paid for the services of the women in some dark recess of the Pleasure Garden seemed shocking – and yet rather intriguing.

How could these two worlds exist side by side – the day-to-day drudgery of life as it had been with her parents and now was with Aunt Hester, and this glittering, sparkling world of silk, lace and tassels? How had she not known? Did this new knowledge come as part of growing up?

Hugh and John called for yet more brandy and sang along drunkenly with Mrs Sorprendo, to the enraged glare of several passers-by who'd come to listen to the famous singer. Even Jacob had drunk too much and was now joining in with his friends, laughing and singing with them rather than talking to Eva.

The behaviour of Hugh and John had become rowdier and Keziah looked at Eva with large eyes and whispered, "Will we go home soon, Evie?"

Henry had already put his arms on the table and despite the noise, he'd laid his head on them and was asleep. Eva realised for the first time she had no idea how to get home and would have to wait for Jacob to take her, but now with his arms around Will's shoulders, he was also singing and swaying in time with the others.

With the shilling Jacob had given Henry, she knew she had enough to get them back to the north bank of the Thames but she'd foolishly not noticed the route they'd taken from St. Margaret's Street. How could she have been so stupid? The glamour of the evening had dazzled her but now, Jacob and his friends' uncouth behaviour had opened her eyes to reality. Eva's stomach churned. How was she going to get Keziah and Henry home safely?

A shrill scream sliced through the music. People paused, heads turning this way and that as they looked for the source of the disturbance. This was a cry of fear, not of revelry. As if by some pre-arranged signal, the musicians increased their volume and tempo, competing with the shouts that came from the far side of the Grove.

"A ring! A ring!" The chant was taken up by other voices, drowning the music.

The milling crowd shifted this way, then that. Indignant dancers left the throng for the sanctuary of their supper boxes while others took their places, elbowing a way through the press of bodies. Every so often, a gap opened and Eva caught sight of two men, one holding his opponent by the lapels, the other, with his fists flailing.

A fight? Eva's stomach lurched. This was not somewhere she should have brought her brother and sister.

'A ring!' The chant grew louder and indeed, there now was a ring around the fighters. Shouts of encouragement. The thwack of fist against chin. Shrieks of delight. Shrieks of dismay.

"Come!" John shouted, "Let's watch! I'll wager a guinea on the chap in the pink jacket! He looks like he knows what his fists are for!"

"Excuse me, mistress," Hugh said, bowing slightly and keeping his eyes firmly on the crowd as he pushed past Eva's chair. The others followed. She glanced at Jacob to see if he was going to leave with them and although he hesitated, he excused himself and said he'd be back shortly.

Keziah, her mouth agape, pressed herself against Eva.

"What's happening?" Henry asked, suddenly awakened by the din. "Can we go and see?"

"No! Certainly not! I don't want you to watch."

But the fight was taking place right in front of them and if Eva took them out of the supper booth away from it, where would they go?

The cheering, jeering onlookers who made up the ring moved with the combatants and were now on the other side of the orchestra. One man was carried out of the crowd with a bloodied face. The other was still standing. He limped away in the opposite direction, assisted by friends. But neither of them appeared to be the original two assailants.

Grunts and blows were still interspersed with cheers and curses. Men and women leaned forward out of upper floor supper boxes. With their unimpeded view from above, they shouted instructions or encouragement, adding to the tumult. Two more men tumbled out of the crowd and fell, struggling together. They rolled, first with one man on top, then the other. Fists thrashed until finally one got his hands around the other's throat. A screaming woman grabbed a handful of his hair, attempting to pull him off.

"Why can't we go and watch?" Henry shouted above the commotion. He clamped his lips shut in a sulky expression.

"No, Henry! Jacob told us to wait here." Eva grabbed hold of his arm to stop him getting a better view.

"No, he didn't! He said he'd come back... And he hasn't."

"But if we get lost in the crowd and he does come back..." Eva paused and tried to slow her breathing. She must not frighten Henry and Keziah with thoughts of being left behind with no idea how to get home.

Keep calm. Keep calm.

Keziah and Henry looked up to her as a mother figure. She must not let them down. If only she could stop trembling.

"It's best if we wait here for Jacob." Eva gently pushed the fringe out of his eyes. He pouted but seemed to accept her words and she reminded herself it was hours past his bedtime and he was undoubtedly tired. Indeed, she was exhausted, having been up since four o'clock.

More soldiers appeared and ran across the Grove. They forced their way into the frenzied crowd which had now spilled out into the Great South Walk.

At the sight of the soldiers, Henry's eyes grew large and he reached out to grab Eva's sleeve. "I want to go home."

"So do I," wailed Keziah. "When can we go, Evie?"

"As soon as Jacob returns, my love." Eva's breath came in short, ragged gasps. Jacob, like his friends, had been quite drunk when he'd left. Suppose he forgot to come back?

Gradually, the soldiers took control and the crowd dissipated. The fight was over.

So, where was Jacob?

Should she go to the Great South Walk and see if she could find them or might they return and, not finding her, assume she'd gone home?

Perhaps she should leave Henry and Keziah in the booth while she went to search but she was reluctant to leave them on their own – and anyway, they were both now almost asleep; Henry with his head on her lap and Keziah with hers on Eva's shoulder. If she tried to move, she'd waken them.

From behind her came the sound of a man clearing his throat. How had he got there without her seeing? Had she fallen asleep? Surely not! How could anyone have fallen asleep at such a critical time? Yes, she was exhausted but this strange feeling in her head was more than tiredness. Had she drunk too much arrack punch, despite Jacob's warning? She'd tried so hard to appear sophisticated and had simply shown herself to be nothing but a foolish child.

"Beg pardon, mistress..." it was the waiter who was clearing the table. "Sorry to disturb you but I must tidy away afore I'll be allowed home. I expect you'll be on your way home any time now... You might prefer to wait at the exit."

Feeling foolish, Eva apologised to the waiter, woke Keziah and picked Henry up in her arms, still asleep. She wondered whether to wait by the exit. Jacob couldn't leave without passing her. Unless there was more than one exit...

As she walked through the Pleasure Gardens, the atmosphere had changed – no longer the frenetic bustle of ladies and gentlemen determined to enjoy themselves – the night's excitement and revels were winding down.

Eva made her way to the exit and was disappointed Jacob wasn't there waiting for her.

Now what should she do?

She followed stragglers from the Gardens to the steps down to the boats and was aghast to see only three watermen waiting. She'd assumed it would be easy to find a boat like it had on their trip across earlier, but the watermen would know that by now there would be relatively few passengers needing their services.

An elderly couple climbed into one boat, the portly man rocking it perilously, as he tried to keep his footing. Eva counted the remaining people in front of her – there were seven. And only two boats left.

All but one lady and her footman stepped into the second boat.

Eva watched in dismay as the last waterman held out his hand to assist the elegantly dressed woman step into his boat. She turned slightly and caught sight of the forlorn group – Eva holding a sleeping Henry, and Keziah clutching a handful of her sister's skirt.

"Pardon me, mistress, but do you have a boat arranged?" the woman waved the waterman's hand away.

Eva rushed to reply, "No, ma'am, I'm afraid we do not."

"Then pray, share mine," the woman said with a brilliant smile and turning to her footman, she waved her fan to indicate he should light their way with his lantern. "Waterman, help my new friends aboard, please."

"Oh! How can I thank you, ma'am?" Eva almost sobbed with relief. "I don't know what we'd have done otherwise."

"Nonsense! No need for thanks. The Good Lord has placed us on this earth to help one another."

Now only a few feet away, Eva could see the woman was older than she'd first thought. Her heavily painted face was decorated with fashionable beauty patches and her hair arranged in an enormous creation through which strings of pearls were wound. But close up, the cosmetics could not disguise the wrinkles at the corners of her eyes and around her mouth.

She'd obviously been beautiful in her youth and even now, she was still handsome – her smile lighting up her face, as she exposed small, white, even teeth. Her intense eyes beneath delicately arched eyebrows seemed to miss nothing.

She held out a gloved hand to Eva. "Please allow me to introduce myself, I am Mrs Henrietta Jenner. And with whom do I have the pleasure of sharing this boat?"

Eva introduced Keziah and Henry who was asleep in Eva's arms with his head against her shoulder.

Mrs Jenner smoothed the skirt of her crimson silk gown with gloved hands, jewels flashing at her wrists. "I trust you've had a wonderful evening, although, I wonder that you've been to such a place unaccompanied... You all appear to be very young."

Eva blushed, knowing it was her recklessness that had resulted in them being in such a predicament.

"Evie's fourteen," Keziah said, glancing at their rescuer in admiration. "And Jacob brought us. But then he forgot us." She scowled to show what she thought of Jacob's thoughtlessness.

"Fourteen, indeed," Mrs Jenner said. "Well, fancy that. You appear much younger!" Eva's cheeks flushed deeper under her scrutiny.

"And I'm sorry to hear you were abandoned." Mrs Jenner's tongue clicked and she shook her head. "Such poor manners. Unpardonable."

Keziah wasn't a child to forgive easily and Jacob's desertion had quickly displaced any feelings of warmth she'd had earlier for the young man. "He left us to watch a fight," she added.

"Ah, I witnessed that spectacle. Disgraceful." Mrs Jenner tutted again.

"And," said Keziah, believing she'd found an ally in the elegant lady in her dislike of fighting, "Evie didn't know how to get home."

Eva gently dug a warning elbow in her sister's side to stop her but if Keziah noticed, she must have assumed it was caused by the motion of the boat which was now halfway across the river.

So, Keziah had known Eva was lost. Somehow, the thought that even her sister realised how inadequate she was, hurt more than Jacob's neglect.

"And where is it you live?" Mrs Jenner addressed her question to Keziah.

Papa had always told Eva not to tell strangers details about oneself. If he'd ever cautioned Keziah she'd obviously been too young to remember the warning. Or perhaps she was overawed with such a fashionable lady taking notice of her and appearing to listen intently to each word. But surely Papa would agree it would be rude to refuse to answer the lady who'd just rescued them from an uncomfortable night on the wrong side of the river.

Think! But the arrack punch had numbed her brain and thoughts were disappearing like water poured on sand.

Keziah said, "After Papa died, we moved into our Aunt Hester's cottage in Calico Alley."

"I see," said Mrs Jenner. "How sad that your Papa died. And presumably your mother also?"

"Yes, when I was four."

"Kezzie!" Eva said in sharper tones than she'd intended, to stop her sister giving more away, "I'm sure Mrs Jenner is not interested in our family history."

Keziah scowled at her.

"On the contrary," said Mrs Jenner pleasantly, "I'm always fascinated to hear about the lives of others. Now, tell me…" She tapped her chin thoughtfully with her closed fan, "Calico Alley. That sounds so familiar. Is it near Mansell Street? Only I shall be passing there on my way home and could perhaps offer you a ride in my coach?"

"It's a turning off St Margaret's Street," Keziah said quickly. Eva had never heard of Mansell Street and doubted her sister had either but she recognised the hope in Kezzie's voice and knew she was wishing it would, indeed, be close enough for Mrs Jenner to take them home.

"I must confess, I've never heard of St Margaret's Street. But then I always rely on my coachman. He'll know where it is and I'll tell him we wish to go there on my way home."

Perhaps Keziah had been wise to tell their new friend where they lived, Eva thought, if it had been left to her, she might have missed the opportunity of a ride home because of her foolish suspicion and would have had to find her way across Westminster on her own.

Nevertheless, she felt obliged to ask, "Are you sure that won't inconvenience you, ma'am?" Next to her, Keziah stiffened.

"Inconvenience me?" Mrs Jenner laughed. "Not in the slightest! We can't have you making your way through the streets of Westminster at this time of the morning. No..." she said with another dazzling smile. "We simply cannot. Now, pray, let us say no more about it. The matter is settled."

Mrs Jenner asked how they'd enjoyed their evening and Eva now forgot her earlier worries and told her about their first impressions – of the magical cascade and the wonderful music and singing.

"And what do you think happened to your young man, Jacob?" Mrs Jenner asked Eva, "I expect he'll be at your front door later, begging forgiveness."

"Oh, he's not my young man." Eva told her about meeting Jacob by chance and how he'd once been her father's apprentice before they'd had to move out of the watchmaker's shop in Black Swan Lane.

"And now your kind aunt has taken you in," Mrs Jenner said.

"She's not very kind," said Keziah, "she's beastly."

"Hush, Kezzie, it was good of Aunt to give us all a home."

Keziah shrugged. "She doesn't like us very much."

"How can that be?" Mrs Jenner's jaw dropped open in surprise, "You are all so delightful!"

"Well, Aunt Hester spends most of her time in bed. She has lots of headaches and she says Henry and I make too much noise. And now our uncle's come home from sea and she sent us out for the evening while she tells him we're living with her and we don't know when we can go back," Keziah said.

"My goodness," said Mrs Jenner tapping her chin thoughtfully with her closed fan; her delicately arched eyebrows drawn together in a frown, "that is indeed a problem but I'm sure when you arrive back she'll be very pleased to see you."

Neither Eva nor Keziah spoke.

"Gracious!" said Mrs Jenner brightly. "See we're nearly there. And just as well, the breeze coming down the river was beginning to chill me." The waterman helped Mrs Jenner out first, then her footman, Charles, to whom he passed the sleeping Henry. Next, he held Keziah's hand and assisted her ashore. Finally, turning to Eva, he whispered, "Watch your step, mistress." He looked meaningfully into her eyes, then opened his mouth to add something when Mrs Jenner called out, "Is aught amiss, waterman?"

"No, ma'am," the waterman said. "Just makin' sure the young lady don't slip, like."

Eva wondered if she'd imagined the urgency with which he'd spoken to her or misinterpreted the message. It was as if he was warning her of something and she was almost certain it wasn't simply to mind her footing.

"Come! Let's hurry! My bed is calling me. You must be tired too, girls," Mrs Jenner said.

Eva had a stab of fear that bed would be denied them if Uncle Will had not agreed to them staying or indeed if Aunt Hester had not yet had the opportunity to ask. How would she even know when it was safe to knock at the door to ask? She'd just have to try it and see what happened.

Keziah and Eva followed the footman who was carrying Henry to the waiting coach where he helped the Bonner children inside. Mrs Jenner had a brief conversation with the driver, then joined them in the luxurious carriage. Eva dug her nails deeply into the palms of her hands as she struggled to keep her eyes open. She longed to let them close and to wake refreshed in a few hours' time to find the nightmare was over and they were safely home in their own bed, with Uncle Will back at sea and out of their lives. Excitement was overrated. She'd be content with boredom and drudgery so long as they were all safe.

Eva woke when the coachman halted the horses and one of the footmen opened the door, allowing in a blast of chilly, dawn air. With a shock, she realised they'd stopped in a grand square – nowhere near Calico Alley.

"Now, Eva, my dear, I hope you don't mind but I thought it best to bring you to my home until a more acceptable time. You can all sleep in Wentleigh House and later, Davenport will take you back to your aunt's."

Eva looked at the large house which Mrs Jenner was indicating and gasped. "I wouldn't want to inconvenience you, ma'am, you've been very kind and I'm so grateful."

"Not at all. Come, my dears! You look as though you're about to drop. Pray, let's make haste."

Eva was too tired to refuse Mrs Jenner's kind offer. Although Henry had slept since they'd got into the boat on the Thames, from time to time he awoke, grizzled and then sank back into a deep sleep. Keziah had woken when the carriage stopped and was snivelling. Eva, too, felt dizzy with tiredness and longed for somebody to take over and put the world to rights. They couldn't be many miles from Calico Alley and yet this grand square lined with mansions felt as remote as the far side of the earth.

Wentleigh House was one of several new Palladian mansions built around a square, in the middle of which was a garden. Eva was surprised to see that behind the drawn curtains, many of the rooms were still lit despite the late hour. Such a great number of candles burning was indeed an extravagance, the like of which, Eva had never seen.

What were all those people doing?

Once inside the large, marble entrance hall, Mrs Jenner was met by several footman and maids who took her cloak and bag. Sounds could be heard coming from rooms which led off the hall – the deep rumble of men's voices, the tinkle of women's laughter, a few notes played on a spinet, the rattle of something which might be dice in a cup – but Eva was too dizzy with tiredness to wonder why so many people appeared to be awake in this house. Keeping hold of Keziah's hand, she followed the maid up the grand staircase, while Charles, the footman, passed Henry to another liveried servant who accompanied them. Charles remained with Mrs Jenner in the hall.

The servant led them into an enormous room containing a bed that was three times as large as the one they shared in Calico Alley. It had heavy, velvet drapes that smelt of rose petals, and an embroidered cover that matched the upholstery on the chairs. The footman gently placed Henry on a chaise longue and when he'd left, Eva undressed him while Keziah took her clothes off dropping them on the floor. A maid pulled back the bedclothes and Eva lifted Henry – still asleep, and placed him in the middle of the bed. Keziah scrambled in next to him. Undressing quickly, Eva climbed in next to Henry and was asleep before the maid had snuffed the last candle.

The sun was extending bright rays through the gap between the curtains when Eva woke, momentarily confused at the light streaming through the strange window. The tiny bedroom in Calico Alley was perpetually dark and since Eva rose before dawn, she was unused to such brightness. Remembering where she was, she sat up quickly, groaning, as pain radiated through her head intensifying with each movement. Waves of nausea gripped her.

Keziah stirred. She blinked several times, looking at Eva in confusion. Lying between the two girls, Henry was still asleep and Keziah raised herself on one elbow. "This is nicer than Aunt Hester's," she whispered, running her hand along the clean white sheet and its lace trim, "I wish we could stay here forever."

"Yes, Mrs Jenner's certainly been kinder than our aunt but don't become too accustomed to the luxury, we must go home today and find out whether Aunt told Uncle Will," Eva said slowly, trying to hold her head still. Every movement intensified the throbbing inside her skull.

"Are you well Evie? You're very pale. Are you sick?"

"No, my love, I'm fine," Eva lied. She was tired it was true, but she was certain she'd inadvertently drunk too much punch and was angry with herself. The pain in her head was her fault. She'd seriously underestimated everything the previous evening. Aunt Hester was hard and uncaring, but she offered them safety from a way of life that last night had seemed so thrilling but this morning was obviously more artificial than the water cascade they'd watched with such fascination. Or, more accurately, Aunt Hester had once offered them safety. That is, until Uncle Will's ship had docked. If he allowed them to stay, Eva must ensure they all kept out of his way. It wouldn't be forever. He'd return to his ship soon and then everything would go back to normal... until the next time he returned. Yes, Aunt would take them back. After all, Eva and Keziah had been useful as unpaid servants and Aunt Hester didn't seem to be capable of running a household.

Eva was just about to drift off to sleep again when there was a light tap on the door and the maid entered with a tray of food which she placed on the table.

"Good morning to you all," she said chirpily as she drew the curtains, flooding the room with light. There would be no more sleep now.

Henry woke and rubbed his eyes. He looked around at his luxurious surroundings with wide eyes, although he relaxed when he saw his sisters.

"Where are we?" He frowned – his last memories were of the Pleasure Gardens and now, he was in a bedroom he'd never seen before. "Where's Aunt?" He glanced around anxiously as if expecting the sour woman to suddenly appear.

"We're going to see her later," Eva said.

"Is that for us?" Henry whispered as the maid began to lay the table. "Can I have something now?" His eyes, at first wary, were now wide in disbelief.

"Where are our clothes?" Eva asked. She was sure she'd picked up Keziah's clothes and left everything on the chaise longue but perhaps they'd slipped to the floor.

"I took 'em to be cleaned," the maid said. "Mrs Jenner is particular about cleanliness. She told me to bring you some clothes until your'n are ready. We didn't have anything suitable which was small enough for the young master and mistress, but the housekeeper altered something, so's they can be decent for breakfast. But we have something that should fit you, mistress," she said to Eva. "I'm Ruth and I'll be back in a jiffy."

The young maid returned minutes later with two dressing gowns which had been shortened for Keziah and Henry. They were much too large but were serviceable once tightened around the waist with sashes. For Eva, she brought a Chinese silk gown.

"After you've broken your fast, I'll fetch you a day frock," she said. "Mrs Jenner chose it. She said it'll suit your dark hair and colouring. But first, I shall draw you a bath. Mrs Jenner is *that* particular about cleanliness." She left to organise the bath and hot water.

"I wish Mrs Jenner was our aunt." Keziah wistfully stroked the soft fabric of her gown.

"I don't want a bath," Henry said.

"We'll do whatever's necessary to please Mrs Jenner," Eva said sharply, regretting her annoyance when she saw Henry's hurt expression.

If only her head would stop thumping.

"I don't mind having a bath," said Keziah. "I wish Aunt Hester would let us bathe more often. Are you sure you're well, Evie? You're screwing your face up."

"Yes, yes, my love, it's just a slight headache. I'm sure I'll be well soon."

"I hope you're not getting one of Aunt Hester's headaches."

"Can we eat now?" Henry asked.

The children had never seen such a sumptuous breakfast. Slices of cold gammon and fresh crusty rolls with rich, yellow butter, honey and coffee. Eva had no appetite but once she'd started eating, she felt slightly better and by the end of meal her head had almost stopped banging.

Two footmen arrived with a bath which they set in front of the fire and several maids filled it with hot water, then brought towels.

Ruth helped to wash and dress Keziah and Henry, and while Eva was bathing, she went to fetch Eva's dress. "You'll love it, miss, it's blue like the sky."

Eva gasped when she saw it. She'd never worn anything so beautiful and she was embarrassed by the extravagant attention Mrs Jenner was lavishing on her. If she'd been wearing it last night, she wondered whether Jacob would have abandoned them. But of course, if she belonged to the sort of family who could afford such a fine day dress, she'd probably have had an elegant evening gown to wear to such social events. Although if her family had been rich, she wouldn't have been in the situation she'd found herself last night because she'd have been accompanied by members of her family and at least one footman, like Mrs Jenner. With a sinking heart, she knew that if she belonged to the sort of family who were respectable, it was unlikely she'd have been allowed into Vauxhall Pleasure Gardens at all. Papa would have been appalled at the risks she'd taken the previous evening.

Keziah and Henry, with their hair still damp, played on the enormous bed, scrambling over it and leaping off. Eva's headache had gone completely and she began to enjoy herself. Ruth gently combed Eva's hair teasing out the tangles and encouraging the natural curl, and Eva hoped the maid would dress it fashionably, piled high on her head, allowing ringlets to frame her face but Ruth was so young – not much older than Keziah, it was unlikely she'd have learned the art of hairdressing. Eva chided herself for being ungrateful. This dress and the attentions of a maid, however young, were more than she'd ever dreamed of.

Ruth was a talkative girl and once she'd got over her initial shyness, she told them about how she'd come to London from Devon with her mother who'd become ill and died. Mrs Jenner had taken the young girl in and was training her to be in service. Eva could see Keziah was taking an interest and idly wondered if perhaps one day Mrs Jenner might take Keziah too. She hadn't given much thought to their futures it had been too much of a trial dealing with the present. Until yesterday there'd been no time for thoughts of what might happen in years to come. Continuing her train of thought she wondered if perhaps Henry might find a post as a footman. And perhaps it was time for her to think about doing something other than keeping Aunt Hester's house – she was educated and could surely find a post working in a shop or going into service like Ruth. Perhaps even becoming a governess. Yes, she liked the idea of teaching. Warmth spread throughout her body. Everything was going to be well. She'd had a warning and it had served to prompt her to think more about the future. And meanwhile, they were all safe.

"There," said Ruth, standing back to admire Eva's glossy, dark hair.

"Mrs Jenner was most particular. She said not to dress your hair. She said you should look young and fresh. And she said once you were ready, to bring you to her rooms." The talkative maid had explained that although Mrs Jenner owned the house, she had the top floor to herself and on the other floors there were many lady guests.

"Is it like a school?" Keziah asked.

"Somewhat," said Ruth vaguely.

Ruth knocked on the double doors at the end of the corridor and at the call to enter, she let the children into a large, beautifully-appointed room. Green damask curtains fringed with gold hung at the large windows and matched the upholstery on the chairs and chaise longue. Eva breathed in the scent of the fresh flowers and hesitated at the edge of the thick rug. It appeared to be too expensive to step on.

Mrs Jenner was seated at a walnut writing bureau, dressed impeccably in a silk grey dress with silver thread that caught the light as she moved. On her head, she wore a matching grey and silver turban with a single ostrich plume.

"Come in, my dears." She rose to greet them and gestured for them to walk across the rug. "I trust you slept well. I'm sure Ruth has been looking after you." She smiled fondly at the young girl who coloured and bobbed a curtsy.

"Yes, thank you, ma'am," Eva said, "you've been so kind."

Mrs Jenner's eyes rested on her for more time than felt comfortable as if appraising her and Eva begin to fidget under her scrutiny.

"That colouring suits you, my dear. You are very comely in that frock."

She clapped her hands together in delight. "Now, I have taken the liberty of writing to your aunt and explaining your plight. Charles will deliver the letter and wait for a response. I trust that meets with your approval?"

"Oh, thank you, Mrs Jenner! You're so kind! I hope one day to be able to repay your generosity," Eva said, grateful for the extra time they'd be able to spend in Wentleigh House.

"Excellent!" Mrs Jenner's face lit up with pleasure. "I'm sure we'll think of some small service you may perform for me. And now, if you'd care to go back to your room, Charles will inform you of your aunt's decision on his return."

Such a kind woman. And yet, Eva was glad to leave her room and escape the intensity of Mrs Jenner's gaze. It had slid up and down her body, seeming to take in every detail from top to toe until Eva's cheeks were glowing. A kind woman – but there was something uncomfortable about her presence.

How ungrateful you are, Eva chided herself.

Charles knocked at the door to their room an hour later.

"I beg your pardon, miss." He looked down as if unable to meet her gaze. "Your aunt said you can't return to her house. Your uncle won't be going to sea for a while and she can't look after you until he's gone. She packed a few things for you." He stood back to indicate a valise and a bag behind him in the hall.

"Oh, my poor dears! What a to do!" Mrs Jenner appeared behind Charles. "I've heard the dreadful news. Well, we simply cannot have you going to the workhouse! No, no! That would be most wrong! Luckily one of my rooms is vacant at the moment, although I have guests coming soon, but I will gladly allow you to stay. Together, we'll think of a plan."

"Oh, thank you, Mrs Jenner, I don't know how we can ever repay you," Eva said, tears pricking her eyes.

"Nonsense, my dear!" Mrs Jenner turned to the footman. "Charles, please take everything to the Orchid Room and ask Ruth to bring our guests some refreshments."

"Yes, ma'am."

"I have an engagement shortly but I'll give your problem the utmost thought, and later, I'll call for you. I'm sure there'll be something we can do which will be mutually beneficial. But in the meantime, perhaps you'll be good enough to remain in your room. I have other guests here who I do not wish to be disturbed."

"Yes, of course, ma'am." There was nothing Eva wanted more than to remain in the one of the beautiful rooms. She felt exhausted after their late night and expected her brother and sister did too.

Charles took them to the Orchid Room. It was decorated in delicate pinks and creams with an enormous bed such as they'd slept in the previous night. There were paintings of orchids and large mirrors in ornate frames on the flock-wallpapered walls, making the room appear larger than it was.

Ruth brought them dinner and when she came to collect the plates, she told them she'd return at four o'clock to take them to see Mrs Jenner. Eva tried to remain awake but when the maid came back, they were all fast asleep. Ruth combed tousled heads and led them to her mistress's study.

Once again, they lined up on the thick rug in front of Mrs Jenner whose gaze alighted on Eva. "I've been thinking, my dear, that perhaps I could offer you all a position in my household. Henry is young but in time, he can train as a footman and Keziah can perhaps become a maid. Eva, I have something special in mind for you. You will, of course, live in the servants' quarters but that will save you any worry about accommodation. What do you say?" She steepled her fingers and peered at them over the top.

"That would be truly wonderful, Mrs Jenner! I cannot thank you enough!"

"That's settled then. Now, return to your room. I shall require you to come later to discuss your work." Mrs Jenner spoke to Eva, "But Ruth will come for you when I'm ready to see you."

The maid led them back to the Orchid Room. As they walked along the corridor, Eva could hear young women's voices and laughter drifting up from downstairs and she wondered what everybody was doing.

When Ruth came to their room a few hours later, Eva and the other two had been asleep again.

"Mrs Jenner wants to see you alone, mistress," she said to Eva, "The training for the young mistress will begin later in the week." She smiled at the sleepy face of Keziah, then turning to Eva, she said, "If you'd like to follow me."

Mrs Jenner was seated at her desk and opposite, sat a small, round woman wearing a plain navy-blue frock with starched white lace cuffs and collar. She smiled but her expression lacked warmth and Eva squirmed under her scrutiny.

"Ah, there you are, dear," Mrs Jenner said when she saw Eva, "I'd like you to meet Mrs Unwin. She's going to be responsible for your training. Now, if you'd like to go with her, she's keen to start immediately. We'll be welcoming some important guests tonight and I'm sure you'll be invaluable, won't she, Mrs Unwin?"

"I hope so, indeed, ma'am," Mrs Unwin rose to her feet with the aid of a black cane. "I hope so, indeed."

Eva wanted to ask what took place in Wentleigh House. She'd assumed it was a school and hearing so many different girls' voices seemed to confirm that. And yet, there were gentlemen's voices too. A hotel perhaps? Could it have two separate functions? And what would she'd be expected to do that evening? Whatever was going on, the house would need cleaning and with a sinking heart, Eva imagined that would be her role. Well, she'd do whatever she was asked. The small round woman with the fierce eyes hadn't given any indication she'd found what she was looking for in Eva and if she wasn't satisfied, the three Bonner children might be turned out.

Mrs Unwin led her down a flight of stairs to a small room furnished with a dining table and she held out the chair for Eva to sit down.

"Observe me well. I'm going to show you how to serve a gentleman or lady and afterwards, I want you to serve me. Is that clear?"

"Yes, ma'am."

"You are required to reach the peak of perfection. Nothing is too much trouble, do you understand?"

Eva assured her she did.

"Our guests' wishes should be fulfilled and if you become good at your job, you'll know what they want before they do."

Eva nodded while wondering how it was possible to know what someone wanted before they knew themselves and why it was so important how she poured brandy and port.

But it was Mrs Unwin's opinion that was vital and the least Eva could do, was her best.

"There will be an opportunity for you shortly to show me how much you've taken in and are prepared to put into action. We have two eminent gentlemen dining here privately tonight and I would like you to serve the dessert and wait until the end of the meal to serve the port. Do you think you can do that?"

"Oh yes!" Eva said, hoping she wouldn't tremble and spill anything.

"You will do exactly as they bid you?"

"Yes, ma'am."

"Good. Then we understand each other," said Mrs Unwin with a doubtful frown. "Ruth will bring you a gown and she'll dress your hair in time for her to bring you to the private dining room, is that understood?"

When Eva arrived back at the Orchid Room, Keziah wanted to know what her sister had learned, and to show her.

"I'm going to be ready when it's my turn." Keziah's jaw set with characteristic determination.

Henry played on the floor with some building blocks that Charles had brought him and took no interest in the talk about serving food and wine.

Ruth arrived with a high-waisted dress of pale blue muslin and matching ribbons over her arm. Eva was disappointed although she tried not to show it and told herself not to be so ungrateful. After all, Mrs Jenner was lending her a dress of much better quality than anything she'd ever worn. But it was nothing like the beautiful gowns she'd glimpsed of the women who were downstairs with their lace shawls and the feathers and elaborate decorations in their hair, and she was even more disappointed when rather than pinning her hair up in an elaborate fashion, Ruth brushed it and allowed the long, dark curls to hang down her back, held in place with just one pale blue ribbon. Several years ago, she'd have been thrilled with this dress. But not now. Eva longed to look sophisticated and elegant.

When she was ready, Ruth took her down to the first floor where Mrs Unwin was waiting in the corridor. She looked Eva up and down with a critical eye, her head to one side like a bird. Her steely eyes hard although there was a slight smile of satisfaction playing across her lips.

"How young you look!" But strangely, this didn't seem to be a criticism.

Mrs Unwin continued, "I cannot stress enough how important it is that the gentleman feel we are making the evening the peak of perfection and to that end, you will do whatever they ask, do you understand?"

"Yes, ma'am," Eva said quickly. She was determined to succeed.

"The slightly older gentleman closer to the fireplace is Sir John Rosecombe and his companion is the Honourable Mr Lansdowne who is about to be elected to Parliament."

Eva nodded. Sir John Rosecombe near the fireplace and the Honourable Mr Lansdowne. She could remember that.

"Are you ready?" Without waiting for an answer, Mrs Unwin raised her cane, tapped on the door and held it open for Eva to enter.

The men's eyes turned expectantly as Mrs Unwin led Eva into the room. It was as the elder woman had described, with Sir John on the left, next to the fireplace and his companion, opposite. Both men were older than Eva had expected. Sir John Rosecombe, dressed in mustard-coloured brocade, leaned back in his chair, his enormous paunch straining at the purple buttons of his waistcoat and his double chin resting on a white stock. His white-stockinged legs extended and crossed at the ankle but when he saw Eva, he sat up and gripped the carved arms of his chair and his languid expression became animated. Mr Lansdowne was younger and more angular with dark, bushy eyebrows in a long, thin face which gave him a perpetual frown and he, too, appeared to inspect Eva. Mrs Unwin stood to one side and after greeting the two men she gestured towards Eva as if she were some new piece of art that was on display.

"Come here, my dear," said Sir John, "how charming to have you serve us." He smiled at Mr Lansdowne and they locked glances.

"An excellent choice, Mrs Unwin, an excellent choice." Sir John's round face lit up and his chins wobbled. "I believe you have reached the peak of perfection, this time. You'll charge it to my account?"

"I say wait a minute, old chap." Mr Lansdowne's dark brows drew closer together to turn the frown into a scowl. "Where are your manners? You haven't given me a chance to bid." He turned to Mrs Unwin. "I'll double whatever Sir John is offering."

Sir John flushed and glared at Mr Lansdowne. "I enquired first. I believe it only good manners for *me* to have the first refusal."

"And I believe I should be allowed to make a bid." Mr Lansdowne lowered his chin and glared at Sir John.

Mrs Unwin rubbed her hands together and looked expectantly at Sir John.

"I've already offered a king's ransom. Surely, you won't forget my loyal patronage?"

"Indeed not, Sir John, but as you've no doubt already noticed, the prize is valuable and not one that is available every day. So many qualities are hard to find at one time. Can I inform Mrs Jenner you have increased your bid?"

Sir John flared his nostrils and appeared to be pondering then with a small gasp of inspiration, he clutched the arms of the chair. "No, I have a better idea we'll let the cards decide."

Mrs Unwin's expression hardened. "I... I wonder if that is indeed seemly," she said hesitantly, obviously reluctant to upset such an important man.

"It's more than seemly," Sir John said. "I'm sure Mr Lansdowne appreciates the assistance I've been able to offer his career so far. A word here, a word there. Words can be so effective, don't you think, sir?" he looked meaningfully at the other man. "Playing for the prize would be a fair way to decide... leaving it to chance, as it were."

Mr Lansdowne tapped one finger on the table and after a few moments of thought, nodded his agreement. His lips were set in a straight line. Mrs Unwin looked from one man to the other but it seemed they'd decided. She withdrew a pack of cards from a drawer and offered them to Sir John on a silver tray.

Once again, Eva was aware of her inadequacy in interpreting this strange world. She couldn't see how whatever was happening could involve her and yet, each person in the room had eyed her with expressions she had no words to describe. Expressions that made her feel very uncomfortable. If she'd dared, she'd have slipped out of the room – perhaps whatever deal they were discussing was not for her ears – she looked at the older woman for a signal to leave, instead, Mrs Unwin said in an oily voice, "Perhaps you would serve the gentleman port, my dear."

Well, that was clear enough.

Eva busied herself with the decanter and glasses, placing them on the table. The two men stared at the pile of cards in front of Sir John.

Mrs Unwin hovered by the door, her hands clasped together on her large bosom as if praying, watching the two men sip port. Sir John finally picked up the pack and shuffled the cards, watched intently by Mr Lansdowne who took one when offered and after turning it over, he laid it down in front of him. It was the five of spades. With a smile, Sir John took a card from the middle of the pack, glanced at it and with a triumphant snort, slapped it on the table. It was the ten of hearts. He clapped his hands together and Eva noticed they were covered in dark hairs – like a wolf, she thought.

Mr Lansdowne stood up abruptly, his chair tipping over backwards and he glanced angrily at Mrs Unwin who rushed forward fluttering her hands.

"We shall make other arrangements for you, Mr Lansdowne, sir."

"See that you do!" he growled.

"Of course, sir! Well, if you'd like to come with me I shall ensure you have the finest evening."

She turned to Eva. "Go with Sir John. And remember all I've told you." She followed Mr Lansdowne out of the room.

"Well, my dear. Fortunate me, eh?" Sir John delicately dabbed the corners of his mouth with a serviette.

"Yes, sir," Eva said wondering if she should clear away the dishes. Mrs Unwin hadn't instructed her on anything other than serving and the only thing she could remember was being told her job was to make everything perfect for their guests. It would soon become apparent what Sir John wanted and if she didn't know what to do, she'd simply have to admit to being new. It wouldn't make her popular with Mrs Unwin but there was nothing else to be done.

"Come, my dear!" Sir John rubbed his podgy, hairy hands together and rose. He walked to the door and when he saw her hesitate, he beckoned with one of his fat, hairy fingers. She followed Sir John along a corridor and into a room which was even more elegant than the Orchid Room. When she was inside, he locked the door.

Keziah wished Mrs Jenner had taken more notice of *her*. The pale blue, muslin dress she'd sent for Eva had been beautiful, and Keziah longed to have something similar. If she behaved well, Mrs Jenner had hinted she would be treated in the same way, and on that day, she'd look as beautiful as Eva. The sisters both shared the same dark, curly hair with copper highlights which the numerous candles and lamps in the Orchid Room lit to perfection. Eva had seemed uncomfortable in the dress despite its beauty and Keziah guessed she'd have chosen something more grown-up such as one of the exquisite gowns Mrs Jenner wore.

"Play!" Henry petulantly pushed a brick towards her, breaking into her reverie. As she reluctantly picked it up, the door burst open and Eva rushed into the room her hand over her mouth and her eyes wide in shock.

"Evie! What's the matter?"

The ribbon which had looked so pretty before, now dangled off the back of Eva's hair which was unkempt as if she'd woken from a deep sleep.

"What happened?" Keziah leapt up and ran to her sister but before she'd reached her, Mrs Jenner threw open the door, her face furious. Despite the white makeup, angry red blotches were visible on her cheeks and her eyes glittered in a way that made both Eva and Keziah step backwards.

With her hands on her hips, Mrs Jenner walked slowly towards Eva.

"Mrs Jenner, I'm so sorry I know Mrs Unwin told me to please Sir John but he... he..."

"*He*!" The word burst from Mrs Jenner's lips with such venom Eva and Keziah stepped back again. "*He* is my most influential and loyal customer and you, ungrateful wretch, you have just kicked him!"

"But he—"

"Enough!" Mrs Jenner held her hand up. "I allowed you to stay, out of the goodness of my heart and you promised to repay me."

"Please! I'll scrub floors—"

"I have enough maids to scrub my floors. What I need is a girl who'll do as I ask."

Eva shook her head. She shuddered and her face twisted in revulsion.

"There's still time to rescue the situation. Sir John's pride has been dented but we could perhaps explain your disgraceful behaviour by saying it was overenthusiastic playacting which resulted in an unfortunate accident. But that may take time. However, I understand Mr Lansdowne was also interested. If you go to him now and behave with more decorum, I believe I could smooth this over. But if not... then you and I can be of no further assistance to each other. Do you understand?"

"But, ma'am, he wanted to—" Eva stopped, looking horror-stricken at Keziah. Her innocent sister must not know what that hideous man had tried to do to her.

"Yes, I know what he wanted to do! You can't be so foolish you haven't worked that out! That is why gentlemen come here. They want to spend time with someone who is well-dressed, well-spoken, accommodating... and particularly... fresh. Surely you understood this?"

"I... I, no, I..." How stupid she'd been! So many things now made sense. The waterman's warning, the men in Wentleigh House at all hours.

"No, Mrs Jenner," Eva said, wringing her hands, "I swear I didn't realise... Please, is there some way I could work for you perhaps in the kitchen—"

"I've told you what I require you to do." Her voice was steely but she added in gentler tones. "After the first time it'll be easier, my dear, trust me. And since you're so young I have many clients who'll be interested in you. Your life could be very comfortable and you'll be able to provide for your brother and sister... if you're sensible. However, if you continue with this very childish and selfish attitude and refused my offer I will expect you to leave immediately. You have five minutes to brush your hair, make yourself presentable and consider your position." She paused and leaned towards Eva until their noses were inches apart. "However, if you refuse... you will find yourself back on the street."

She turned abruptly and strode out of the door, the feather in her hair bobbing.

Keziah gasped. What on earth had Eva done to anger Mrs Jenner or indeed what had she not done? Surely, Eva would see sense? She wouldn't allow them to be thrown out.

"Evie! You must do as Mrs Jenner tells you!" Keziah grabbed her sister's arm. "Haven't you've always told me to obey your betters?"

But to Keziah's dismay, Eva merely sobbed into her hands.

"I can't!" she said between her fingers, "I simply can't!"

"Well, if you won't, I will!" Keziah stamped her foot. This was her chance to show Mrs Jenner *she* was worthy of beautiful clothes and ribbons.

"No!" Eva said with such vehemence that Keziah flinched.

What had got into Eva? She was usually so sensible.

"I'm sorry, my love, but I can't explain." Eva wiped her eyes with the back of the hand. "Keziah, you *will* listen to me! If the choice is that we do as Mrs Jenner asks or we're told to leave then we must leave! I'm sorry, but that's how it must be."

"But why, Evie?"

"I can't explain," said Eva wretchedly. "You're too young!"

"I'm always too young!" Keziah stamped her foot in frustration. Why hadn't Mrs Jenner asked *her*? She'd have obeyed!

At the door, Charles, the footman, cleared his throat. "I'm sorry, miss, but Mrs Jenner sent me and if you won't do as she asks, I'm afraid I must take your bags down to the street."

Keziah wailed and Henry began to sniffle. The footman hesitated. "Just a minute or two more, miss. But if I were you, I'd think very carefully..."

"Please, Evie!" But Keziah could see her sister was going to ruin everything.

Eva looked at Keziah and Henry, their eyes wide, in faces white with shock. She couldn't speak for the enormous lump in her throat.

To have explained how stupid she'd been would have meant telling them what she now understood about this house and Mrs Jenner's business. The desperate, bedraggled women who touted for business in Covent Garden had been easy to spot with their heavy makeup and lewd language and behaviour. It had only needed Betsy to explain what went on after one of those women encountered a willing customer for Eva's eyes to be opened.

But Betsy had never pointed out any well-dressed, seemingly refined ladies plying the same trade. How had Eva been so foolish? Especially after seeing Jacob's friends. But those women had never been part of her life, how could she have been dragged into theirs?

The opulence and glamour of this particular house had fooled her completely and she'd only seen the exquisite gowns and the expensive furniture and it hadn't occurred to her this was an exclusive bawdy house which operated along similar lines to the low-class ones Betsy had told her about in Covent Garden.

But now she knew the truth, she had a choice – she could either go to Sir John or Mr Lansdowne... and... her imagination failed her. But if she refused, they'd all be turned out onto the street.

"Can I help you do it?" Keziah asked, desperately. Her eyes full of tears.

"No!" Eva said sharply making both her brother and sister jump. The tears Keziah had been fighting to hold back flowed down her cheeks at the sharp retort and Eva stepped forward to put her arms around her shoulders.

Keziah shrugged her off. "Don't!" She wiped her eyes on her sleeve. "If you're not going to do whatever Mrs Jenner wants, then don't pretend you care about Henry and me because you obviously don't!"

"I do care!" Eva covered her face with trembling hands.

At the door, Charles cleared his throat, interrupting them. "I'm sorry, miss, but Mrs Jenner wants to know if you've changed your mind..."

"No! I'm sorry but I can't do it." It sounded as though the words were being torn from her.

Charles nodded slowly and regretfully.

"It's not too late!" Keziah grabbed Eva's wrist as Charles picked up their valise and bag.

"I can't do it, I simply can't!"

"Can't?" Keziah's lip curled in contempt. "*I* can't believe you're being so selfish! You're always telling me off for thinking of myself and now you're doing just that! What can possibly be that bad?"

Keziah's words and her look of contempt stung. Perhaps she *was* being selfish. Couldn't she go to that man? Close her eyes. Pretend she was somewhere else. Endure. And keep a roof over their heads. Her skin crawled at the thought of his touch. Her stomach heaved. No. She simply couldn't do it. There must be another way...

"Where will we go?" Keziah demanded, pulling Eva's arm.

"I don't know," Eva said quietly, "I don't know." She closed her eyes and wished the world would go away. This was too hard.

"Haven't you got any family, miss?" Charles asked.

"Only Aunt Hester," Keziah said, "But as you know, she doesn't want us."

Charles swallowed, his cheeks reddening. "Is there no one who'll take you in tonight?"

Eva shook her head.

"Then..." He paused as if weighing up whether to speak. "I... If you've got nowhere else to go, my sister'll give you a roof... for a couple o' nights. D'you know Chalk Lane?"

"Yes."

Who hadn't heard of notorious Chalk Lane near the stinking River Fleet? Betsy had repeatedly warned Eva to avoid it, and the courts and alleys that led off it. But anything would be better than being on the street. Perhaps on the morrow, they'd find their way back to Calico Alley and throw themselves on their aunt's mercy.

"My sister lives in Drovers Yard, off Chalk Lane, near the King's Head. Her name's Nancy Allenson. Ask anyone. Everyone knows Nance. Can you remember that?"

"Yes, thank you," Eva nodded gratefully. "You've been so kind to us, Charles."

He pulled at his collar and looked away as if unable to meet her gaze, then he picked up their remaining items.

"Not that way," he said as the children turned towards the main staircase, "We have to use the servants' stairs."

Halfway along the corridor, they passed an elderly gentleman with a young girl on his arm who stopped to peer at the group through his jewelled lorgnette. Mrs Jenner, who'd been checking the Orchid Room was empty, rushed towards him, "Lord Magnan! How marvellous to see you again! I trust Therese is entertaining you to your satisfaction?"

"Get them out of here!" she whispered to Charles, her voice low and angry when Lord Magnan had gone. "We're not running a nursery!"

Charles led them out of the servants' entrance. "Turn left at the corner, keep going until the end, then turn left again and sooner or later, you'll end up in Chalk Lane. Good luck and I'm sorry... I'm deeply sorry."

"My boots are rubbing my heels," Henry moaned.

"Evie doesn't care," said Keziah with a toss of her head.

Eva remained silent. She wasn't sure where they were, only having been along this road before with Papa in a hackney carriage on the rare occasion when he'd taken her with him to deliver a watch to a wealthy client. She wasn't sure where they should turn off nor who she could ask. Around her, the sounds of London clamoured – girls calling out to men to buy a posy for their lady, pie sellers with delicious-smelling wares which reminded Eva she had very little money for food. She hoped Henry wouldn't complain of hunger. It gave her no satisfaction to know his blistered heels were taking his mind off his empty stomach.

Ahead, two sedan chairs had stopped and the chairmen were shouting at each other to get out of the way. One lunged for the other and they fell to the ground, fists flailing. Heavily laden with the bags, Eva shepherded the children across the road away from the crowd that was already gathering but Keziah pushed her away angrily.

"I can manage," she said crossly.

Eva fought back the tears but holding tightly on to them both, she found a way across the road through the line of waiting hackney carriages and sedan chairs. As they reached the other side, Eva heard a shout from behind which penetrated all the cries of encouragement to the fighting men and the scream of a woman who'd been jostled.

"Mistress Eva!"

She turned and saw Charles, the footman, his face flushed. He was gasping for breath. "Wait, Mistress Eva," he said, "I'll take you to my sister's room. It's the least I can do."

Eva looked at him gratefully. The crowd had grown and there was no way to pass.

"You owe us nothing," Eva said. "You've been so kind. Won't you get into trouble with Mrs Jenner?"

"I've finished work for the day." Charles swallowed and looked

44

down. "Come with me, I know a way through the alleys to Drovers Yard. We won't get through that mob."

He led them down a side street and stopped. "I *do* owe you something, miss. I sincerely beg your pardon. If it hadn't been for me, Mrs Jenner wouldn't have found you at Vauxhall Gardens."

"But if she hadn't found us," said Keziah, "we'd have been left on the other side of the Thames."

"And that letter I delivered to your aunt didn't ask if you could return," Charles continued, "Mrs Jenner told her you'd be working for her and paid a sum of money in compensation. Your aunt'll have to pay it back if you go home. A man answered the door. He took the letter and shortly after your aunt put the bags outside the door."

The lump in Eva's throat threatened to choke her. She simply stared at the young man. If she'd felt foolish before, this was the final insult.

"So, you drew Mrs Jenner's attention to us at the Pleasure Gardens and then she targeted us and paid our aunt so she wouldn't allow us back?" Eva could barely push the words past the lump in her throat.

"You must understand, it's my job to look out for girls for Mrs Jenner. I'm paid to do that. Mostly, they're grateful. Mostly, they take to the work after a while. I didn't know you'd be different..."

Eva silently stared at him. What was there to say?

"When will we be there, Evie?" Henry glanced from his eldest sister to the young man who'd earlier given him building bricks.

A passing dog began to sniff at the bag Charles was holding and he jerked it upwards.

"Get away with you!" Charles aimed a kick at the animal who backed away snarling.

"Here, miss, allow me to carry the young man," he said picking up Henry. "Now, if you'll come with me."

Silently, the two girls followed him. Keziah stared stonily ahead as she marched behind Charles. Inside Eva's chest, her heart was breaking.

Nancy Allenson was nothing like her younger brother, Charles. She didn't resemble him physically, nor indeed in temperament and kindness. She greeted him with a grunt and a complaint that he'd neglected her recently and then another complaint that the bones in his bag were not very numerous, nor meaty.

Nancy dropped the bones in a pot, then added water and placed them over the fire in the hearth.

"You want me to look after the lot of 'em?" Her mouth twisted into a sour expression as she looked at the three newcomers.

"They're desperate, Nance."

"And how much'll they pay me?"

"I thought they could help you... Make themselves useful, like. It'll only be for a day or two."

Nancy glared at her brother from beneath heavy eyebrows that were drawn together. "You're asking me to take them in for nowt?"

"I reckon if somebody does you a good turn," said Charles, his tone now steely, "then you ought to do the same for someone else, don't you?"

"You help me out once and then you don't never let me forget."

"It's not like I'm asking for anything for meself, Nance. I'm just asking you to do something nice for once."

"Are you sayin' I don't ever do nothin' nice?"

"Please..."

"I'll need money..."

Charles reached into his pocket and withdrew a shilling which he held out to her.

She snatched it.

"So, you'll look after them for a few days?"

Nancy's mouth set in a straight line. She clenched her jaw and turned back to the pot to stir its contents. Finally, she said, "They can stay but don't expect anything much, I ain't got nothing to spare. An' one shilling won't go far."

"I'll work hard," said Eva. "If you'd be so kind as to take us in. We'd all work hard, wouldn't we? And hopefully, we can go back to our aunt's soon." She looked at Keziah and Henry, hoping they'd both agree.

Henry nodded and Keziah, obviously realising this was the only option, managed a sulky, "Yes."

Charles refused any soup and said he needed to get back to Wentleigh House.

"Good thing he ain't stayin'," Nancy said when he'd gone. "He don't come round for months and then only brings a few bones." She dropped several potatoes and some cabbage into the thin, greasy soup. Eva hoped neither Henry nor Keziah would complain but it seemed the repulsive Nancy Allenson had intimidated them both. As soon as the meal was over Nancy told Eva to clear up while she went out for a few hours.

"Make yourselves at home," she said, with a sweeping gesture of her hand.

Nancy rummaged through a pile of rags and pulled out a cloak. "Have you got any money? I'll get some food if you have."

Eva gave her the coins Aunt Hester had given her.

"Is that all you've got?"

"Yes, I'm sorry."

Eva looked at her in disbelief, she was nothing like Charles. Or perhaps the poverty in which she lived had shaped her, whereas Charles's life in Wentleigh House, was much easier.

Nancy put on the ragged cloak and as she left, she said, "The bed's mine. Don't touch it. There's some sacks in the corner. Make yerself up a bed out o' them."

"I'm tired," Henry said his eyes brimming with tears. He watched in silence as Eva laid out the sacks on the floor and tried to arrange them into something that approached comfortable for them to lie on. Eva dozed fitfully waiting for Nancy's return. She hoped Nancy would bring something for them to eat for breakfast. The bone broth had been thin and unsatisfying.

Nancy returned as the first glimmer of grey dawn light struggled to penetrate the filth on the cracked window of the room. Either she'd forgotten she had guests or she didn't care because she staggered into the room, tripped, cursed and finally lay down on her bed fully clothed. Seconds later, she began to snore. The stuffy room filled with the stench of gin.

When there was enough light to see, Eva got up and quietly began to clean the room. Keziah lay with her face towards the wall her eyes closed. Her body was rigid and Eva suspected she was awake and trying not to cry. Henry was still asleep and Nancy's snores filled the small room. She lay on her back, her mouth open and Eva couldn't help watching the slack jaw in the ferrety face, open and close, open and close.

When Keziah and Henry were both awake, they watched Eva search for food, with resignation in their faces, until finally, Nancy woke up. She peered vacantly at the children as if she'd forgotten they were there, then she groaned and clutching her head, she sat up. "What are you lot gawpin' at?" Her face contorted with pain and she groaned again.

"Did you buy breakfast?" Eva asked, knowing the woman hadn't brought anything back with her when she'd returned. She squeezed her fists tightly, hoping desperately Nancy hadn't spent all the money.

"Ain't we the lady then?" Nancy sneered. "If yer want breakfast, love, you better go and buy it."

"I gave you all the money I had."

Nancy laughed, her lips drawn back to show her black teeth. "Welcome to my world."

"But you said you were going to buy food," Eva said.

"Well, it looks like I changed my mind. If I'm going to look after every waif and stray, I need some sustenance."

"Did you spend all the money on gin?" Eva asked fearful of the reply.

"Who are you? Me mother?" Nancy unsteadily got to her feet and jabbed a finger at Eva. "I can spend me money on what I like."

Eva was silent. There would be no point angering Nancy further. If the money had gone, it was too late to do anything about it.

"I'll take the young'un out shortly and we'll bring something back won't we, dear?" she smiled at Keziah.

"No!" said Eva. "I'll come with you. She can look after Henry."

Keziah leapt to her feet. "I'm old enough! And I'm just as much use as you... I'm probably even more use!" Her tiny fists were clenched and her eyes blazed.

"She's got spirit!" Nancy laughed. "I'll take her."

With a triumphant glance at Eva, Keziah picked up her cloak and swung it around her shoulders, then followed Nancy out of the gloomy room. She threw a look back over her shoulder as if to say *you're not capable Eva, but I am*. As the door slammed, somebody in a nearby room swore loudly and a baby woke up and cried.

When Nancy and Keziah returned, the older woman was smiling. "Get it out then, girl."

Keziah pulled out a loaf and three apples from beneath her cloak and placed them on the table. Her face was white and she avoided looking at Eva.

"She's a natural!" said Nancy. "And she's got the looks of an angel."

Out of her pocket, Nancy withdrew three silk handkerchiefs, a watch and a satin, lady's purse. She held up the handkerchiefs and inspected them. "Should get five pence each for them down Whitecross Street. And a couple o' guineas for the watch. Now, what've we got in 'ere?" She loosened the drawstring on the purse and tipped out several coins which spun on the grimy table. Placing her fingertip on the guinea, she let the pennies come to rest on their own, then she pushed them towards Eva.

"Go and get some food." She smiled benevolently, then looking at her haul, she added, "I'm going out to sell these little beauties."

As soon as Nancy left, Keziah burst into tears. "She made me steal, Evie! Reverend Peters said thieves burn in hell. Am I going to hell?"

Eva wrapped her arms around her sister. "No, my love. I know you wouldn't have done that on your own. I don't think God will hold it against you if you were forced to do it. It's Nancy who's the thief."

"Let's get the constable." Keziah scrubbed the tears from her eyes with clenched fists, her face screwed up with determination.

"No, Kezzie! We must be careful! If the constable arrests Nancy, you might be taken too!"

Keziah's face turned white. "But you said God wouldn't hold it against me!"

"God may not but I'm not sure what the law would say, Kezzie. We need to think carefully."

"We could try Reverend Peters at St Margaret 's Church," said Keziah. "He knew Papa and Mama. He'd take us in, wouldn't he?"

"If we go to Reverend Peters, he'll let the parish know we're homeless and they'll almost certainly send us to the workhouse."

"Wouldn't that be better than being here?" Keziah's face lit up with hope.

"Not if they split us up."

"Why would they do that? We're a family. They'd keep us together."

"No, I don't think they would. Men and boys go into one part of the building and the women into another."

"Well, we could ask if we could stay together. They'd surely listen."

"I don't think they would."

Keziah snorted and rolled her eyes to the ceiling in frustration.

"That's what I've heard, Kezzie." There was no point arguing with her sister. They all needed to work together.

"Well!" snapped Keziah. "You probably haven't heard right!"

Eva ignored her sister's rudeness. "Henry, my love, please give me that shilling Jacob found in your ear. I need to buy food." Then turning back to Keziah, she added, "Please keep an eye on Henry and I shall be back soon. While I'm out, I'll try to think of a way we can all stay together."

Keziah waited until she could no longer hear Eva's footsteps, then told Henry to be good.

"I'm going out for a while," she said.

"Don't leave me, Kezzie!"

"Do as you're told! I'll be back soon."

Keziah put on her cloak and let herself out of the room onto the stinking landing and carefully made her way downstairs, checking Eva was out of sight. She ran out of Drovers Yard into the busier Chalk Lane and stopped a woman who was passing.

"Excuse me please, ma'am, I need a constable do you know where I could find one?"

"A constable you say? Now why would you need one o' them, my dear?"

"There's a lady who lives in there." Keziah pointed at Drovers Yard. "And she just made me steal something."

"Steal something? Did she now! Well, fancy that. You wouldn't know the name of this fine lady, would you?"

"Nancy Allenson."

"Ah, Nance..." The woman nodded.

"Do you know her?"

"Oh yes." The woman smiled, revealing blackened teeth much like Nancy's. "I know her very well. So, you're after a constable, are you, dearie?"

"Yes." Keziah backed away slightly. The woman hadn't reacted with outrage as she'd expected. She'd even seemed amused, as if she approved of Nancy Allenson. Well, if this woman wouldn't help, then Keziah would find someone who would.

Before she could turn away, the woman said, "Leave it with me, dear, I'll call the constable right away, don't you worry."

Despite the reassuring words, there was something in her face and expression that disturbed Keziah. But at least she'd said she would fetch the constable and once Keziah had a chance to explain what had happened... Then what? Her breath caught when she realised there was no proof of the theft of the handkerchiefs, pocket watch and purse because Nancy had taken them with her. Well, no matter, the constable would be able to see she was telling the truth. Honesty would always win out.

Keziah quickly made her way back up the stairs, holding her nose as she trod carefully, avoiding the detritus on each step. Henry gasped with relief when she came back into the room. He was still sitting near the fire where she'd left him, his nose running and his eyes red.

"Kezzie!" he sobbed and wiped his eyes on his sleeve.

"I told you I wouldn't be gone long!" Guilt at leaving him alone made her tongue sharper than she'd intended. And it wasn't simply guilt at abandoning Henry. Worry gnawed at her. Had she done the right thing asking that woman to send the constable? Suppose she forgot? Or had lied? Keziah shouldn't have trusted her. She should have... Well, it was too late now, there was no time to go out and find one herself because Eva would surely return at any moment. Her chance had gone.

By the time Eva had returned with milk and cheese and had given them all something to eat and drink, Keziah's stomach was a hard knot of anger and disappointment. Why had she relied on that woman? She should have done the job herself.

Eva kept aside a portion of food for Nancy, then they tidied away and still, the constable hadn't come.

At noon, Nancy returned, clutching a bottle of gin. With glazed eyes and a lopsided smile, she staggered across the room, lay down on the bed and before long was snoring.

"When can we go?" Henry whispered, echoing Keziah's thoughts.

A loud hammering on the door woke Nancy, who propped herself up on one elbow and blinked. "Open the door afore it gets broke in!"

It was the constable.

Keziah squeezed her hands together in delight. Now Nancy would have to answer for her crimes. Keziah's hand unconsciously went to her ear. It still throbbed where Nancy had twisted it so hard, she'd screamed. After Nancy had slapped her hand over her mouth and whispered threats in her other ear, Keziah had agreed to do as she was told.

Her heart had hammered in her chest as she'd walked up to a gentleman that Nancy had pointed out, and politely asked him the way to Holborn. He'd leaned over so that his face was level with hers and while he'd been directing her; his bony finger pointing out the way she should go, Nancy had bumped into him and walked on. He'd grunted with indignation, brushed himself down and resumed his bent position to finish directing Keziah. Then, he'd smiled, told her to take care and had crossed the road. For a second, she hadn't known what to do until Nancy had appeared from nowhere, seized her arm and dragged her into an alley.

Nancy had pushed Keziah against the alley wall and twisted her ear again. "Don't just stand there after I've lifted something. Walk quickly away and follow where I go."

Keziah later learned that in the split second that Nancy had barged into the gentleman, she'd dipped his pocket and taken his watch.

Nancy had then taken Keziah into the marketplace where she'd pretended to trip. She'd tumbled headlong into a woman who was waiting in the baker's queue and they'd both fallen against the table of loaves. Keziah knew Nancy wanted her to snatch any from the ground and conceal them beneath her cloak but she was trembling so hard, her fingers wouldn't obey her. She'd grabbed two loaves, dropped one and almost lost the other before she finally tucked it beneath her cloak. She'd stood there, then, struggling to breathe until Nancy nudged her and jerked her head for Keziah to follow. The enraged baker's shouts had roused Keziah and she'd fled, panic spurring her on to run faster than she'd ever run before. Legs pumping and lungs bursting.

On her way through the crowd, Nancy grabbed a few apples off a stall when the shopkeeper's back was turned and after leading Keziah into a dingy alley, she passed them to her to hide beneath her cloak.

And now, after such a terrible morning, when the constable came, he'd arrest Nancy and remove her from their lives. Admittedly, Keziah hadn't considered the problem of where she, Eva and Henry would go, but common sense told her the parish would look after them. After all, Papa had paid his rates promptly and had also given alms to the poor. Now Papa's family would surely be looked after.

"Nancy, Nancy!" the constable said in mock disapproval. "What on earth 'ave you been up to now?"

"Up to? You know me, John! Honest as a new-born babe!" Nancy winked and laughed.

Keziah's eyes swivelled from one to the other – this wasn't how she'd imagined the conversation would take place. It was as if they knew each other.

Eva put her arms around Keziah and Henry. The arrival of the constable was not welcome at all. But hardly surprising considering the sort of life Nancy led.

"That's not what I heard, Nance!" The constable tutted and shook his head in mock disapproval. "I've 'ad reports of allegations of theft and I 'ave to take allegations seriously, as you well know."

"Allegations, is it?" Nancy's cold eyes flashed with fury and she glared at Eva who returned her gaze. She certainly hadn't spoken to anyone about Nancy. Alerting a constable would have risked them being turned out of Nancy's room – as grimy and neglected as it was. Even worse than that, it might have implicated Keziah. She glanced at her sister and was shocked to see a lack of surprise at the appearance of the constable and even a hint of triumph. Had Kezzie slipped out of the room and talked to someone while Eva was buying milk? She'd certainly have had time. But why had she disobeyed Eva?

"Damn you!" Nancy screamed at Eva, "I take you in from the bawdy house and you try to get *me*, an innocent woman, into trouble!"

"I didn't! I promise I didn't speak to anyone!"

"It wasn't Evie! It was me and you're not as honest as a new-born babe!" Keziah shouted. "You made me take that loaf! And you stole a watch and a purse!"

All eyes now turned to Keziah. Eva gripped her shoulder tightly but she twisted away, then stood, hands on hips, her face defiant.

"The child's nothin' but a liar. You don't believe her, do you, John?" Nancy's voice had risen slightly.

The constable crouched in front of Keziah and spoke in a kindly voice, "Are you telling me you stole a loaf, young mistress?"

Eva stepped in front of Keziah. "My sister's done nothing wrong."

"Well, somebody has." The constable stood up and looked down at Eva. "There've been accusations and I 'ave to look into them."

"I believe there's been a mistake, Constable. My sister is confused."

"She's confused all right." Nancy sniffed.

"Even so," the constable said, "allegations 'ave been made in public so I 'ave to be seen to be doing something or who knows where it'll end. A body won't be free to walk the streets without felons attacking 'em. So, if the girl says items have been stolen, I 'ave to follow it up, see?"

"I can see yer problem, John, so I'm going to be honest with you. An' I 'ope you'll take into account my previous good character..." Nancy took his arm and stroked it.

Could this be true? Was Nancy about to admit to taking Keziah out to steal things? She certainly looked as though she was trying to get on the right side of the constable. Perhaps she was hoping he'd let her off if she was honest with him.

"I don't like to peach on anyone. Specially not a child. But I swear on my life she's got the lightest fingers I ever seen. Just you look at this..." Nancy reached under her bed and pulled out the turquoise silk lady's purse. "She tucked this under the bed afore you came in, John. On my life, she did."

Keziah spluttered with indignation and Eva reached out to put her arm around her.

Please, Kezzie. Don't say anything.

But it seemed that Keziah had no words. Beneath Eva's arm, she was shaking.

The constable whistled with admiration.

"Well, that definitely don't look like it belongs to you, Nance!" he said with a laugh. "And you're tellin' me the girl stole it?"

"Brazen as you like. Boasted about it she did. Bold as anythin'."

"I didn't steal that! *You* took it!" Keziah pointed at Nancy.

The constable held out his hand for the bag. Nancy passed it to him.

"That seems straightforward. Now, miss, if you'd like to come with me." The constable placed a large dirty-fingered hand on Keziah's shoulder.

Eva pushed between them. "Please, Constable, my sister didn't take anything." Eva fought to keep the panic out of her voice.

"She's already admitted stealing a loaf and now we 'ave a witness to another theft. As I said afore, I think it's all quite straightforward. Now if you'd step out of my way, miss."

"No! You can't take her!" She grabbed the man's hand and tried to prise it from Keziah's shoulder.

"I think you'll find I can." The constable's voice was steely. "And if you don't get out of my way, I'll arrest you too." He shoved Eva, knocking her to the floor.

Henry clung to her crying.

What should she do? How could she choose? It was impossible. She couldn't let him take Keziah. Neither could she get herself arrested with Keziah and leave Henry alone with Nancy.

Think! Think!

"Wait! Please, Constable! How can I make you understand there's been a mistake? My sister is honest, she'd never have deliberately taken anything."

The constable said nothing, merely raised his eyebrows and held up the purse by one of the cords. He shook his head, then pushed Keziah towards the door.

"Take me instead." Eva turned to Keziah. "Look after Henry, Kezzie. Keep him safe."

The constable jutted out his lower lip as he looked from one girl to the other. He shrugged. "I don't much care who I take, but I don't want to hear no more accusations." He pushed his face towards Keziah's until it was inches away. She recoiled; her eyes wide with fear.

Please, Kezzie, don't say anything.

Thankfully, she remained silent.

"I trust I'll hear no more about thievin'." His nose was still level with Keziah's.

There was now no trace of defiance in Keziah's eyes – simply fear.

Surely the constable would take pity on them. Wasn't it obvious Nancy was lying?

But if it was, he didn't want to know. His bony fingers dug into Eva's arm. "Now, you, come along with me."

Keziah and Henry clung to Eva sobbing.

"You might as well take them all, John. They're a family of vipers. I took 'em in, out the goodness of me heart and see how they repays me. I don't want 'em here in this honest home spreading their lies."

"Where will you take them?" Eva wrapped her free arm around Keziah and Henry.

"The parish'll send 'em to the workhouse," the constable said matter of factly, picking Henry up around the middle and seizing Keziah's arm. "But you'll be comin' with me."

Eva followed them down the stairs.

Two of the constable's men were waiting in Drovers Court and he directed them to take Keziah and Henry to the workhouse.

They clung to Eva, grabbing handfuls of her skirt and cloak but the men grew weary and eventually seized each child with a strong arm around the middle and wrenched them from her. Henry screamed and bit the officer's hand and Keziah's fists pummelled the other man, but they were carried away; arms flailing and legs kicking.

A crowd gathered to watch the spectacle and call out advice to the constables. But no one stepped forward to help

"Kezzie! Henry! I love you. I'll do what I can to get you out!" Eva shouted so loudly, her voice cracked.

Their screams were the only reply.

Eva tasted blood on her tongue and realised she'd bitten so hard on her bottom lip, it had bled.

"Please! They're only young. Please let me go to them!"

"Don't worry about them," the constable said, pushing Eva through the crowd, "you're the one in trouble."

Chapter Four

Weeks rolled into months, until Eva, Kathleen and the other women who were going to be transported to New South Wales were loaded onto the outside of stagecoaches to travel down to Portsmouth. By the time they arrived, they were filthy, chilled and soaked through as it had rained heavily on the last day of their travel. The dishevelled group were hustled along by soldiers towards the waiting ship, the *Lady Amelia*.

Men nimbly swarmed up the rigging, while others peered over the side of the ship, staring at their new cargo of prisoners. Some were laughing, others appeared to be discussing the bedraggled women in the queue, pointing with fingers or pipes and leaning forward for a better look at the wretched creatures who'd begun to file up the gangplank.

Many of the women gripped the rope handrail with both hands – unused to the rocking motion of the ship. Others, who refused to step onto the bucking ramp, were pushed forwards by the soldiers, impatient to finish the job and leave the stormy dockside.

Eva held her cloak tightly around her as the freshening breeze with its salty tang, plucked at the fabric, trying to tear it from her body. With one hand she clasped the front edges together and with the other, she held the rope tightly as she made her way up the gangway towards the jeering sailors onboard the ship.

The women were led below and assigned one of the cramped berths that lined the sides of the low-ceilinged prison deck. There was no light or ventilation in the oppressive deck and quickly, the temperature rose with so many women packed together. With the increased heat, the smell of unwashed bodies intensified.

Kathleen and Eva had been separated as they were herded to the prison deck so they had been given berths several yards apart until Kathleen asked the woman next to Eva if she'd exchange places. The woman was obviously unaware of Kathleen's reputation but it didn't take her long to realise it was best to do as Kathleen requested. She muttered to herself as she staunched the blood flowing from her nose and made her way to her new berth.

Kathleen had instructed Eva to tell people they were sisters. They would explain the difference in accent and surname by saying their mother was Irish, their father English. When the family had split up, their father had returned to England and taken his younger daughter with him, leaving his wife and elder daughter in Ireland. So far, if anyone had disbelieved the story, they'd not had the courage to say so. And as

Kathleen pointed out, "Why should anyone care?" But it would be easier for her to look after her 'younger sister' should the need arise.

The rocking motion of the ship increased and several women were heaving over the buckets at the end of the deck, adding to the already unbearable stench. The unfamiliar pitching motion and the cramped conditions were causing problems, even amongst the women who'd become used to the harsh prison environment. Further along the deck, red-haired, fiery Mary Norris who'd failed to subdue Kathleen in prison, took offence at something, or perhaps simply wanted to establish her authority over her new neighbours. With a curse, she lunged at a woman, knocking her to the floor where they writhed; punching and kicking.

An officer blew a whistle, summoning two red-jacketed marines who barged through the throng and grabbed the two flailing assailants, dragging them apart. One of them roughly hauled the nearest woman away with his arm around her neck. She scrabbled at it ineffectually with her fingers. Her opponent, the red-haired aggressor, had been pinned to the deck while the soldier shackled her wrists behind her back.

The officer shook his head in contempt. "Put the pair of them in irons to cool off." He held a handkerchief to his nose and waved his men away. Then calmly, he continued to allocate berths to the line of women who were still pouring onto the lower deck while Mary was hauled away, screaming abuse at the soldier who dragged her up the ladder.

Eva lay on her cot and closed her eyes, trying to control the waves of nausea which were washing over her. They were still in the harbour and it wasn't very rough – but she was finding the rolling motion nauseating. If it was like this now, how would she cope when they were on the high seas?

There was a commotion at the far end of the prison quarters – heavy footsteps on the deck above, accompanied by deep voices which increased in volume as men climbed down the ladder to the prison quarters. Eva raised her spinning head far enough to see the master of the ship and several of his officers holding lanterns aloft to inspect their new cargo.

The ship's master, Edgar Yeats, was small and portly with a stomach so large, his waistcoat appeared to be at bursting point. His booming voice carried down the aisle to the far end of the deck. "The lanterns will be removed at eight o'clock each evening and there will be no leaving this deck until morning. As for meals, your berths are arranged in groups of four and you will eat with those in your group. One woman will be chosen from each group to be mess steward and to go on deck and bring back your rations, morning and evening. While at sea, you will have the use of the poop and quarterdeck during the day and exercise will be allowed during clement weather. Needless to say, I expect you to obey my officers at all times. Misdemeanours will be treated with the utmost seriousness and rigour, and if the need arises, I will have no compunction at carrying out the death penalty. Already two of your number are in irons. There they will remain until I see fit to release them. I will not tolerate brawling, neither will I countenance lewdness or immorality aboard my ship."

Eva noticed Kathleen's face was contorted with contempt as she observed the master and his officers. It was an expression Eva had seen on Kathleen's face while she observed the turnkeys or constables and on the one occasion when Kathleen had spoken about the counterfeiting gang to which she'd once belonged. None of them had been arrested, yet only one of them had ever visited her or helped her. It seemed Kathleen despised men, although, Eva conceded, none of the men she'd encountered since she'd been arrested had been worthy of respect. Indeed, Kathleen displayed a lack of respect to everyone – male or female – except to Eva. Kathleen's late sister, as well as resembling Eva, shared her name, although it was the Irish *Aoife* which Kathleen pronounced softly, as '*Eefa*' and those coincidences appeared to have favoured Eva with the older, tougher woman's guardianship.

Captain Yeats concluded his talk to the laughter and derision of several of the women who yelled obscene comments. With great dignity, he ignored them and led his men to the cooler, fresher upper deck. Eva laid her head down, closed her eyes and wondered how long it would be before the nausea passed. The creaking of the ship's timbers, the shouts of sailors above and the wailing and retching of the women around her assaulted her ears – and the reek filled her nostrils.

Kathleen regularly brought her water from the bucket at the end of the deck. It smelt and tasted as if it had been drawn from a pond.

"Just rest, *Mavourneen.*" Kathleen trickled water over Eva's face to cool her down. "To be sure, you'll feel better in a day or two."

A day or two? Eva was appalled. How was she going to bear this dreadful churning in her stomach and the dizziness? And after she felt better – assuming that she ever did? Months of living in the stink and heat of the prison deck stretched before her.

The *Lady Amelia* ploughed through the heavy swell off the coast of Portugal before Eva began to feel better and was able to keep down a little of the food Kathleen brought her. She felt light-headed and weak as she went up onto the open deck for the first time to exercise with the other convicts in the fresh sea air.

Captain Yeats and the government agent, Lieutenant Brooks, oversaw the milling group of women from the elevated poop-deck. Nevertheless, sailors and marines glanced appraisingly at the women when they thought they were unobserved by the master, and many of the women returned their interest. Most of them knew what the men wanted and were willing to offer it in return for companionship, money or favours.

The officers had taken their pick of the women, some taking housekeeper lovers and others going so far as taking 'sea-wives' – including the handsome government agent, Lieutenant Brooks who Kathleen said, had taken a young girl to his cabin before the ship had even set sail.

"She's no criminal," Kathleen commented. "She's too soft. Like you, Mavourneen. She's not guilty of anything. But a pretty wee thing like her wasn't going to have to bide long for a man to claim her. I hope that officer is good to her. At least she's got herself out of this rat's hole. But the minute she's with child, he won't want to know."

After that, Eva noticed when any of the ship's company or marines tried to catch her eye, Kathleen would make it clear their attentions weren't welcome.

"Don't let them get their hands on you, Mavourneen, they'll use you and then when it suits, they'll desert you." Kathleen's lip curled in scorn. Eva found it easy to keep out of the men's way. She cut her hair short to keep down the lice and she was always in Kathleen's shadow. If she was alone, she kept her eyes down and didn't engage any of the men in conversation. There were plenty of women on board who wanted the men's attention – and the business – so Eva's lack of interest in soldiers and sailors went unnoticed.

The *Lady Amelia* was expected to arrive in Santa Cruz, capital of Tenerife, within the next few days and there was great excitement because Captain Yeats had said the convicts would be allowed to disembark with an escort of marines. He was proving to be a tolerant and considerate ship's master. Others in charge of convict transport vessels had operated a harsher scheme, shackling prisoners together and not allowing them as much access to exercise in the fresh air as the women of the *Lady Amelia* enjoyed. A trip ashore would have been unthinkable for them.

The thought that Eva's life might contain something enjoyable hadn't occurred to her. The immediate future was to be endured until she could make her way home again after existing for seven years in a place she couldn't begin to imagine. So, she was pleasantly surprised to discover she was looking forward to the prospect of disembarking in a different country.

However, tensions had been mounting on the prisoner deck where Mary Norris had been trying to establish her importance and had decided the only person who was a threat to her authority was Kathleen O'Marne. Not that Kathleen was concerned. People knew not to aggravate her but several of the women who'd been tormented by Mary were keen to pay her back and saw Kathleen as their champion. So, when Mary provoked Kathleen, the others were quick to react, and a vicious fight ensued.

The scratched, bruised and gouged women were quickly separated and put in irons to calm down and for the first time on the voyage, Eva was alone. As soon as Captain Yeats learned of the brawl in the prison quarters, he imposed a ban on any of the women leaving the ship to go ashore in Tenerife.

Eva watched enviously as the ship's crew who weren't on watch climbed into the longboats and rowed to the harbour for a night of entertainment and fun. Not that she yearned for either, but having grown excited at the prospect of seeing somewhere new and exotic, it now seemed unnecessarily cruel to dangle it in front of her but not allow her access. Would this run of bad luck ever end? Or was this how her life was destined to turn out – disappointment after disappointment, as Fate crushed the life out of her? The sun set rapidly and as darkness fell, lights began to twinkle in Santa Cruz which appeared even more enchanting than it had in the sunlight. The wind shifted direction, blowing from the shore toward her, carrying guitar music and singing.

"'Tis a beautiful place," a voice from behind her said, making her jump. She turned to find a junior officer leaning against the animal shack behind which she'd hidden.

"'Tis a great shame you'll miss out because of a few headstrong, savage women," he added.

He was taller than her and slightly older – perhaps seventeen, she guessed – almost a man but the down on his upper lip and the hesitant smile still proclaimed his youth. Had he been a man, she'd have immediately excused herself and squeezed past him to keep out of his way. Most of the men aboard, assumed all the convict women were available for their use – for domestic chores and for their pleasure although most of them, so far, had accepted Eva's rejections with mild annoyance and perhaps a curse or two. But this young man seemed to be well-bred, from his voice and manners, and she smiled at him and replied that Santa Cruz was indeed unlike anything she'd ever seen.

"I'll wager you'll like Rio de Janeiro," he said, his hesitant smile becoming more confident. "Let's hope you get the chance to see it."

"Is it like this?" She pointed towards the shore.

He considered for a moment, a slight frown on his forehead as he thought. "I'd say it's similar but much better. Of course, that may be because the voyage from the Canary Islands to Rio is a long one and everyone is much relieved to see land. Perhaps that's what makes Rio seem more pleasurable. But to me, it seems livelier and more colourful. Of the two places, I favour Rio."

"How many times have you visited?"

"Only once before, on another ship. And I've been to the West Indies several times. But New South Wales'll be the furthest I've ever been."

She sighed. How marvellous to have travelled and seen so much of the world. "I've only left London once, to go to Essex," she said, "hardly any distance at all."

"Not to Ireland? And yet I believe your sister speaks with an Irish accent."

"You're very well informed!" How did he know so much about her?

"I've seen the two of you together and your sister's gained notoriety for her part in the last fight. So, are you sisters?"

Eva's cheeks reddened as she lied. "Yes. Our family split up. Kathleen stayed with our mother. My father brought me to England when I was a baby. We grew up apart for many years." How she hated lying about her relationship with Kathleen – it seemed so disloyal to her own family to deny their existence. But Kathleen had been adamant this was the best thing to do and after all, what did this young officer care if her parents had been happily married and her real sister and brother were now in a workhouse?

He nodded as if accepting her story but his half-smile suggested otherwise.

"Well, it's nice to have made your acquaintance... Miss?"

"Eva Bonner."

"Midshipman Jeremy Findlay," he said with a polite bow and then turning on his heel, he walked off and left her.

Strangely, she realised she was disappointed he'd gone.

Kathleen was released and returned to the prison deck, but almost immediately came down with the bloody flux, and Eva, having managed to keep out of everyone's way while her protector had been gone, now despaired she would die. Three women had succumbed to the disease so far.

It wasn't just that Kathleen was Eva's protector, she'd become more than that – possibly even turning into the elder sister they were pretending she was.

Kathleen didn't gossip and she spoke sparingly, but she'd taught Eva much about the world and in particular about men. She had very little time for them having been let down many times including by the man she'd loved and the gang to which he belonged.

She'd taken no part in the counterfeiting procedure although her man had persuaded her to return the forged coins into circulation, promising as soon as he'd made enough, they'd marry and buy a shop. However, before that could happen, the operation had been reported to the authorities, possibly by someone who had eyes on the market the gang currently monopolised. When the officers raided the gang's workshop, pouches of coins had been pressed on Kathleen who tucked them into her clothes. She was therefore implicated in the crime although while she was being searched, several of those who'd carried out the counterfeiting, had escaped through one of the back doors into the warren of alleys outside. Only one of those who remained free had taken the trouble to find out how she was and to pass her some money – the money she'd used to find out where Keziah and Henry had been taken. And that man had not been her lover.

Now Kathleen's life was in jeopardy. She burnt up with the fever and became weaker and weaker, despite Eva bringing her water to cool her down. But each day as they approached the Equator, the stuffy, sweltering heat of the prison hold increased and became more oppressive. Sails had been rigged on the upper deck to act as fans and to attempt to blow air into the lower decks to increase ventilation. Nevertheless, the temperature soared. Eventually, Kathleen was taken to Surgeon Dawson's cramped hospital where Eva was not welcome. The low-ceilinged room was small and there was barely room for the patients.

The weather alternated between intense heat and violent storms and even worse, they were becalmed for two days without a breath of wind – the sails barely flapping – and those which had been rigged to cool below decks, were useless. But despite the oppressive heat, Kathleen began to recover.

During a dry spell, Captain Yeats ordered the convicts be brought to the upper deck and Surgeon Dawson oversaw the cleaning of the prison quarters with liberal amounts of antiseptic oil of tar, to attempt to control the outbreak of the bloody flux. The precautions appeared to work because no one else succumbed, and the sick gradually recovered.

One day, several weeks after they'd left Tenerife, Eva could tell something had changed. There was an excitement in the air which was infectious. One of the women told her the ship would reach the Equator later that day and the crew would mark the crossing with a ceremony. Eva couldn't imagine what the Equator looked like, nor how it was marked. Would there be something like a ribbon across the sea to show where the Equator lay? And if so, how would the ship sail through it?

"Bless you, dearie!" The woman smiled and patted Eva's arm. "There ain't no mark!"

"Then how do the sailors know where it is?"

"They just knows." She shrugged, and Eva suspected she had no idea either.

Just before midday, the prisoners were allowed on the upper deck and they joined the crowd of sailors, who, judging by their faces knew what was about to happen. Eva tried to persuade Kathleen to go with her to the top deck to see the Equator but she said she was tired and wanted to rest, and anyway, she didn't think it sounded very exciting. But Eva couldn't resist joining the women, although she kept to the back of the crowd and spoke to no one.

"Hello, again." It was Midshipman Jeremy Findlay, who'd slipped through the crush, and was now next to her. His boyish smile lit up his face.

"You won't be able to see anything," he said, dragging a crate over for her to stand on. He took her hand and helped her up and then to her embarrassment, kept hold of it.

"We can't have you falling overboard."

"What's going to happen?" She turned her face from him to hide her flaming cheeks.

"It'll start any time now."

To her surprise, he was peering along the deck and not out to sea where she'd expected everyone to be looking – towards whatever marked the Equator.

"Over there!" he said. "Look at George! He's playing Neptune!"

A man wearing a loincloth, a long, false beard and a crown on top of a wig made from rope strands elbowed his way through the crowd. In his hand, he carried a trident which he waved, to the delight of the sailors and officers. He was followed by another crew member who was dressed in women's clothes with a neckerchief tied to hide his hair and beard. He also wore a crown and both men were soaking wet.

George jumped onto a large crate and with his huge fists resting on his hips, he surveyed the crowd with mock severity. "I am King Neptune, arisen from the ocean! And this, my lady wife, Queen Amphitrite. Or as I call her, Mrs Neptune." The crowd whistled and roared as George heaved his companion, who was hampered by his skirts, onto the crate. "Bow before me, subjects!" He swiped at the sailors who'd gathered around the crate, with his trident.

"I've risen from the sea to chastise and initiate those who've never crossed the line before. Bring them before me for sentencing!"

A dozen blindfolded sailors were brought forward and George interrogated each in turn, sentencing them to give up their rum ration for a week or be ducked in a large pool of seawater on the main deck.

One by one, the blindfolded sailors were thrown in the pool and ducked before being allowed to clamber out and celebrate with extra rations of rum.

Finally, King Neptune announced that all hands had been initiated into the rights and privileges owing to his subjects and that the ceremony had drawn to a close.

"Did you enjoy it?" Jeremy asked Eva, helping her down off the crate and still keeping hold of her hand.

"Yes! I hadn't expected anything like that."

"I was ducked on my first voyage," he said, "the crew always look forward to crossing the line but this time with all the women, it's going to be a rare celebration!"

Already, several of the seamen were tuning up musical instruments, with the unspoken approval of Captain Yeats, who watched from the poop-deck with several of his officers. Sailors and convicts began to dance.

"Will you perhaps dance with me?" Jeremy smiled at her shyly.

"I... I don't know how to," Eva admitted and looked down, feeling rather foolish. He placed his finger under her chin and tipped her head up. "I'll show you. Come! No one'll notice if you get the steps wrong."

He led her to the edge of the twirling dancers and she watched his feet and tried to copy. Several couples left the crowd, hand-in-hand, and slipped away past Jeremy and Eva. He smiled and winked knowingly at her. "Cap'n Yeats is turning a blind eye to the happenings of tonight!" he said. "Perhaps he's taking his orders from King Neptune!"

The beat of the music became more frenetic and the dancers spun, keeping pace. Eva suddenly realised Jeremy was looking over her shoulder and she turned to follow his line of gaze. There was a strange light out at sea.

No, not a light exactly, more of a glow.

"Come!" Jeremy said, his eyes alight with excitement. He took her hand, pulling her along the deck, away from the dancers. At first, she tried to pull her hand away but when he turned and looked at her, she saw his boyish excitement, and she was caught up in his enthusiasm. He nodded to her encouragingly and she followed. Ahead, further along the deck, the government agent and his sea-wife were sharing an intimate moment, their attention on something over the side of the ship, so, Jeremy led Eva to the other side, away from the couple.

"Let's not disturb them."

With both hands on the gunwale, he leaned over and looked down, then glancing back at her, he beckoned for her to do the same. She stood on tiptoe and peered at the sea. The water was glowing with a beautiful, shimmering, blue light. As the bow of the *Lady Amelia* sliced through the water, creating waves that surged away from the ship, their crested tops were iridescent with the blue colouration.

"What is it?" She gasped and leaned further over to get a better view.

"I don't know. I've heard of it but never seen it before. Some say it's caused by tiny creatures in the sea but that doesn't seem likely to me. Others say mermaids are lighting candles below the water."

Suddenly there was a disturbance about fifty yards away as fish leapt out of the water, their bodies flashing blue and green in the moonlight before they dived back into the shimmering sea.

"Bewitching!" The warmth of his breath was on her cheek and she knew he wasn't referring to the shimmering colours in the sea.

She turned towards him, their faces inches apart. Hesitantly, he leaned closer and placed his hands gently on her shoulders as if afraid she'd push him away. But she didn't want to push him away. She longed to be wanted and there was no doubt Jeremy wanted her.

It seemed as if the world had receded – the music and singing faded into the distance, drowned by the sails flapping and the waves slapping against the hull. It was almost as if she and Jeremy were alone on the ship in the middle of the ocean. He gently drew her towards him and at the first touch of his lips on hers, shivers of pleasure ran through her body.

Her first kiss.

She was so light-headed, if it hadn't been for his arms holding her tightly, she felt as though she might float up into the velvet, star-sequinned night. Never had the world felt so magical.

Was this what other women felt like before they coupled with a man? Was this what drove them to the frantic fumblings in dark corners which she'd considered so undignified and even sordid? How could it be? There was nothing immoral about this.

His hands stroked her neck, straying into the short-cropped hair, sending waves of pleasure coursing through her and if his mouth hadn't been over hers, she would have moaned with delight. She could feel his strong muscles pressed against her curves as she moulded into him. He kissed her neck and she threw her head back as he slid his finger beneath her kerchief, moving it to one side to make way for his lips. A sound pierced the distant strains of fiddle and pipe and the cheering of the dancers. A voice. Urgent. Outraged.

"Aoife!"

It was Kathleen.

Jeremy slid his arm around Eva's shoulders and gripped her tightly.

Kathleen, panting with exertion, stood with hands on hips her face a mask of rage and disgust. "Get your filthy hands off her!" She seized Eva's wrist and pulled her from his clasp.

"I thought I'd shown you to behave better than that!" Kathleen's eyes were narrow slits as she regarded Eva.

Jeremy stepped forward and squared up to Kathleen, his fists bunched. "Why don't you go back to the hellhole where you belong? This has nothing to do with you!"

"If you place a wager on my sister's debauchment again, and I'll kill you!" Kathleen's voice was low and menacing.

She saw anger flash in Jeremy's eyes as he turned to Kathleen. "She's all yours then!" He shoved past them and walked off along the deck.

Still weak from her illness, Kathleen was caught off guard and fell heavily against the gunwale. She regained her balance and glared at Eva, then clearing her throat she spat overboard into the shimmering, blue ocean as if to taint its beauty. Turning on her heel, she marched back to the prison deck. Eva followed, pulling her kerchief back into place. She held her head low, imagining everyone could see her shame.

Could it be true? Jeremy had wagered money she'd give herself to him? Disappointment crushed the air from her lungs and she struggled to breathe.

But how would Kathleen know? She must be wrong...

"I keep my ears open," Kathleen said as if she'd read Eva's thoughts.

The following morning, Eva found Kathleen staring over the side of the ship at the water which last night had been brilliant and iridescent. Today it reflected the leaden clouds overhead which promised a heavy downpour.

"I'm sorry," Eva said simply. She'd rehearsed several apologies and explanations but really there was none. Kathleen sadly shook her head still staring down at the grey water with the lacy foam. "Yes, Mavourneen. It's always the way – sorry after the pleasure. I thought you'd be wiser than that..." She sighed. "But you're still young. You haven't seen enough of this world yet."

Eva bit her lip. Had she been forgiven? Or should she try again? But what more was there to say? She was sorry she'd let Kathleen down and had fallen short of her hopes and expectations. There was no going back and changing that. And she was sorry she'd once again been used. It wouldn't happen again. She gripped the gunwale until her knuckles turned white and stared at the dull, foam-flecked waves. No, she wouldn't let it happen again.

Would Kathleen forgive her? Eva would do her best to win back her trust. So far, the only trustworthy person she'd met since her father had died, was Kathleen. Eva would not give up the friendship without a fight and if that meant keeping as far from all the men, including Midshipman Jeremy Findlay, for the rest of the voyage, that was fine. She certainly had no desire to see him again.

As the days passed, Kathleen who was still recovering from her illness, remained weak and it became clear that she – like Eva, and many of the other people aboard the ship were showing signs of scurvy since the fresh food they'd loaded in Tenerife several weeks before, had long since run out.

Life lapsed into a monotonous regime for Eva with the ship's bell ringing out the watches as one day merged into another. She began to wonder if Kathleen had forgotten about that night at the Equator because she'd never mentioned it again.

A few days later, the *Lady Amelia* arrived in Rio amidst much excitement and this time the convicts were allowed to go ashore accompanied by the soldiers but Kathleen still hadn't recovered from the bloody flux and had been weakened further by scurvy. She didn't want to go ashore and Eva stayed aboard too. She watched the women climb into the longboats and gazed longingly at the city of San Sebastian de Rio de Janeiro but although she longed to see it for herself, she also knew she owed Kathleen her loyalty and anyway, who would she go with? She had no friends and the prospect of exploring a foreign city on her own was daunting indeed. Lights began to twinkle in windows as the sun abruptly dipped below the hills. As the darkness grew, the chirrup of insects drifted across the still water carried by the evening breeze with a mingling of exotic, spicy scents. She and Kathleen sat on the deck, their backs to the shore, discussing what their lives might be like in New South Wales.

The first time she and Kathleen set foot on the ground during the voyage, was in Cape Town. The large square opened off the harbour but according to Sarah, another of the convicts, it wasn't as interesting as the streets of Rio with its statues of Virgin Mary on many corners and large squares full of exotic flowers.

"Cape Town belongs to the Dutch, you see," Sarah said knowingly as if that would explain all.

But Eva was glad to have disembarked at least once on the journey although the strange rocking sensation she'd felt on what she knew to be solid ground, was quite unnerving.

"It's good to be on land," observed Sarah who was voicing the opinions of the sailor with whom she was now attached. "My John says we won't know what's hit us when we reach the Roaring Forties."

But further questioning revealed that Sarah had no idea what the Roaring Forties were, nor what to expect. However, it soon became obvious, when the *Lady Amelia* reached the latitudes between forty and fifty degrees south of the Equator and experienced the howling wind and tumultuous seas. Eva felt violently sick again as did many of the women and she remained in the stinking, confined convict deck, hanging on to her cot. The ship ploughed its way through the ocean barely surviving the wrath of the Roaring Forties and entered Antarctic waters. The sea, still raging, found its way into the ship through various cracks and holes drenching everyone, and chilling them to the bone.

"Please let it be over!" Eva heard someone wail as if praying, and she wondered if the woman was asking for an end to the voyage or simply an end. It would be a sin to beg for the end of a life, Eva thought and then immediately wondered why. After all, her life was now meaningless – she could do nothing about the people she loved, she'd let down the only friend she had and she was bound for a place where she'd heard life was so hard, people died of starvation or were eaten by savages.

The *Lady Amelia*, however, survived and as it rounded Van Diemen's Land and turned north towards Sydney the weather improved. The coastline appeared similar to England although here and there along the beach and at the edge of the forests, pinpricks of fires could be seen and when the weather was clear, long coils of smoke rose upwards which, it was whispered, were the fires of the savages who lived on Van Diemen's Land. Eventually, under brilliant blue skies, the ship sailed between the two headlands into Port Jackson, finally dropping anchor in Sydney Cove.

Chapter Five

Adam Trevelyan sniffed the air appreciatively. The wind carried the faintest hint of wood smoke and the sharp, sweet scent from the eucalypt trees towards Sydney Cove, dispersing the unpleasant smells of humanity emanating from the colony. The town was busier than when Adam had last been there. Not surprising because periodically, convict ships arrived, disgorged their human cargo, and then shortly after, returned to England via China or India. But few of the people living in Sydney enjoyed the freedom to leave on those vessels. One day when Adam had saved enough money and had his Absolute Pardon, he'd be one of those passengers who'd board a ship bound for England.

Now, from his slightly elevated position, he surveyed Sydney Town. Since he'd last been there, the people had changed. They'd hardly be described as prosperous, but the hunger and deprivation which had typified the colony when he'd last seen it was beginning to fade, and with it, the pinched faces and air of desperation.

Adam had played his part in relieving the food shortages. He'd used the farming knowledge he'd gained on his father's estate to help the settlement farm to maximise its crop yield and to keep stores safe from the many unfamiliar pests the new colonists encountered in New South Wales. The governor had been pleased with his hard work and had assigned him to Mr Pritchard, a freeman, to work on his farm in Parramatta. Adam had been told that assuming he kept out of trouble, after a few years, he'd be eligible to receive his ticket of leave, after which, he'd be allowed to work for himself, and even to acquire property, on the condition he reported regularly to the magistrate. Any misbehaviour would result in the ticket being withdrawn but Adam hadn't had any intention of letting that happen.

However, nothing had gone to plan. Adam bit his lip as he remembered – berating himself once more for his foolishness in allowing Philip Turley to goad him into losing his temper. He eased the breath out which he'd been holding and willed his fists to unclench in the way he'd trained himself to do since the day he'd punched Turley. True, the man had been offensive and had deserved it but Adam should've curbed his temper. And what poor timing! Two more weeks and Adam would've had his ticket of leave and been able to set up on his own. Instead, he'd been bound to Pritchard for a further year. But Adam had sworn he'd never lose control again. After that, he'd reined in his hot temper and in five months, he would gain his ticket of leave.

Nothing would get in his way this time.

Mrs Pritchard was a problem. She was several years younger than her husband and she'd made it clear to Adam she'd taken a fancy to him. Not that he was interested. He'd no intention of risking his ticket of leave a second time. Adam ensured he was never alone with her and was usually as far from the Pritchard's house as possible. Take today, for example, despite the scorching sun, he'd volunteered to drive the cart to pick up supplies with Mr Pritchard, rather than remain on the farm near that woman while her husband was away. The last thing he was looking for, was romantic entanglement – not after Rosenwyn.

He'd once been placid to the point of indolence probably because there'd been little in his life to fire his anger. But the circumstances surrounding his arrest and the shock of the death sentence which had been commuted to transportation had robbed him of his easy-going nature and had fuelled his fury. All Adam cared about now, was returning home to Cornwall with sufficient funds to run his father's estate.

But that wasn't all. He yearned to expose Mr Hugh Pengelly to the Cornish society he'd tried so hard to join. And as always, when he remembered that man, his mind was filled with images of Pengelly's daughter, Rosenwyn. He felt the usual stab of pain as, in his mind's eye, he saw her beautiful face framed with blonde curls, and as he'd forced himself to do over the years, he replaced visions of her with thoughts of his Absolute Pardon and of returning home, a fiercer but less gullible man.

Adam still burnt with the injustice of Hugh Pengelly's deceit which had resulted in his arrest for smuggling, and his loss of Rosenwyn. How could Adam have been so foolish as to believe that if he took part in a smuggling operation, Mr Pengelly would look favourably on his proposal of marriage to his only daughter? Mr Pengelly might not have the ancient pedigree of the Trevelyan family but he had plenty of money. It wasn't sufficient on its own to buy him a place in Cornish society – but with Rosenwyn's beauty, he was determined to achieve an alliance with a family who possessed both breeding and riches.

Adam's father, Joshua, had suffered various financial setbacks. Two of the family's copper mines had begun to fail and a fire had gutted one wing of their home. On the day Adam had called to ask for Rosenwyn's hand, Mr Pengelly had made it clear that despite being Joshua's heir, he was not wealthy enough to be worthy. Unless...

Mr Pengelly admitted he had a problem because one of his ships was due home the following day after a short voyage to France to stock up on brandy, wine, silks and lace. Tom Roach, who usually organised the unloading of the cargo and its storage, had been arrested by the Preventative Men the previous week and Mr Pengelly was finding it hard to replace him at short notice with someone trustworthy. He knew Roach's trial would result in a fine – after all, he hunted with the magistrate, Robert Morcrombe. Mr Pengelly would secretly pay the fine to free Roach but that would be too late for the arrival of the cargo.

Smuggling was an accepted way of life in Cornwall, everyone knew that. And it was only the occasional customs man who took the job seriously. If you knew the right people, it was no threat at all. Mr Pengelly wondered if perhaps Adam could find his way to manage the merchandise – just this once – and then he might look more favourably upon the young man's proposal.

And Adam had fallen for it. He'd waited on Henvallen Beach the following night with a few of Mr Pengelly's men and several mules.

The ship never arrived.

The excise men, however, did.

Against all odds, Mr Pengelly's men escaped and the only person who was arrested was Adam Trevelyan who was tried by Magistrate Morcrombe and found guilty of smuggling goods which had been discovered on several of the mules. Very strange because the cargo had been landed several miles away.

Too late, Adam realised he'd been a decoy to keep the excise men busy, but worse, someone had deliberately planted the smuggled goods to incriminate him. The judge condemned smuggling and felt dutybound to make an example of young Trevelyan, accordingly, sentencing him to hang. However, Joshua wasn't without friends amongst those with some authority and eventually, his son's sentence was reduced to transportation.

Never again would Adam be so trusting. And never again would he fall in love. Rosenwyn had refused to see him – that had undoubtedly been her father's doing. It had been the letter her maid had delivered that had broken him. It was a letter that Adam was certain her father knew nothing about. In it, she apologised for not informing him in advance and telling him she now couldn't possibly consider any sort of friendship with a criminal. After the love he'd believed they shared, he'd assumed she'd wait for him. Now, he realised she must have known of her father's scheme but hadn't attempted to warn him.

How little he'd known of life. And of women.

Rosenwyn. The name that had once made his heart beat faster now curled his lip in scorn. He had no need of a woman.

One day Adam would buy into a business, work hard, then sell up and make his way back to England where he'd... Adam never let his imagination to go any further because there was no point making plans when he had no idea about what was happening at home. Letters from Cornwall arrived rarely and the news was always months old. Lives could change in the blink of an eye. His father had been healthy when Adam had left but that was nearly three years ago.

The blink of an eye, he thought as he swatted a fly away from his face. How true that was and he cursed himself once more for his foolishness in allowing Philip Turley to goad him.

Adam batted another two flies away. Where was Pritchard? Sweat dribbled down his back. He'd found a shady place under a tree but the sun had moved since he'd first taken shelter and soon he'd have to seek shade somewhere else. Knowing Pritchard, he was in the local alehouse making sure he had plenty to drink before the return journey.

Finally, Adam spotted his master coming along the road. His progress was slow and he meandered slightly, suggesting he had indeed been to the tavern. Pritchard wanted another farm labourer and having heard of the arrival of a convict ship, had arranged the trip to Sydney but now, following him was a young girl. She was so thin it seemed like a puff of wind might blow her over. Adam frowned in disbelief. They didn't need a skinny girl, they needed a strong man to help with clearing a new bit of land.

Tears glistened in the girl's large, red-rimmed eyes and threatened to trickle down her hollow cheeks. Having recently arrived on the convict ship, she would be starving, scorbutic, lice-infested and probably have very few morals, Adam thought and then reminded himself he considered himself to be honest and that not all convicts were criminals. ·Some had merely been desperate. And this one had an air of desperation about her now.

"Let's go," said Pritchard, his speech slurred, "Put 'er there." He indicated the girl should sit between them in the cart.

"She tried to run away afore. Can't have her escaping. Not that there's anywhere to hide but we don't need the aggravation." Pritchard shoved her into the middle of the seat.

With her skinny elbow sticking in his rib, Adam could feel the tremors as she fought back her tears. Pritchard nodded off, his chin on his chest and his head bobbing as the cart bumped its way along the dusty road. Adam didn't want to risk waking him so he remained silent throughout the journey and indeed, what was there to say? There was nothing he could do for her. No point comforting her, he wouldn't be around to look after her and it was best she fended for herself.

Nevertheless, it was hard to ignore her distress.

When they arrived at the farm, Pritchard awoke and getting down from the cart, he ordered the girl out.

"Go into the house, girl. I'm sure Mrs Pritchard will find you plenty to do."

His wife waited patiently by the door. She smiled at Adam but he busied himself with the horse, then he led it away, leaving the girl standing there.

CHAPTER SIX

"I'll find you, Mavourneen! Don't lose hope!" Kathleen had cried before a man clapped a hand over her mouth and dragged her and Eva apart. At the same time, Pritchard had seized Eva firmly around her upper arm and wrenched her away from Kathleen's clasp.

All hope had gone. Nothing mattered anymore. Nobody cared if Eva was separated from Kathleen, the woman who'd treated her like a sister nor whether she'd ever see her real brother and sister again. No one cared she'd been convicted of a crime she didn't commit. All those things were so vital to her, yet meaningless to anyone else. She was hollow. Empty. Nothing.

Her new master led her away and Kathleen's screams were stifled as she was dragged in the opposite direction.

On arriving at the Pritchard's farm in Parramatta, Eva's new mistress had been less than welcoming, demanding why her husband had returned with a feeble-looking girl and not a strong hand for the fields.

"I was misinformed. The ship only carried women." His tone was sufficiently angry to stop his wife making further comment.

Later, when Eva got to know her vain mistress better, she realised the displeasure Mrs Pritchard had initially displayed had arisen from jealousy because she was no longer the only female on the farm. However, when she saw how Eva went about her work, so carefully and quietly that it was easy to forget she was there, Mrs Pritchard relaxed and began to enjoy having a servant. The relationship wasn't an easy one. Polly Pritchard was naturally envious and Eva made a point of being unobtrusive.

She lived for the day she'd receive her pardon and then she'd find a way of returning to England to find Henry and Keziah. Although she wondered if either of them would remember her by that time, particularly young Henry. She had to believe they were still alive. There had to be something to hope for.

"Bring more bread, Eva." Mrs Pritchard carried the stew to the table and served her husband. She sat down opposite him. "Wouldn't it be fine, to have a separate dining room?" she said wistfully. "Real gentle folks have a separate room and someone to serve meals."

Pritchard merely snorted and grabbed the bread which Eva placed in front of him. "All in good time." He took a large bite of bread and chewed with his mouth open.

"But you said it would be soon..."

"I know what I said! But I'm not made of money!"

Mrs Pritchard toyed with a piece of carrot. "But you said the farm was doing well." Her tone was accusing.

"And so it is but these things take time. If I'd been able to get a man instead of... her." He nodded his head towards Eva. "Things might've been better. P'raps I'll take her back to Sydney the next time I go..."

"Oh no!" said Mrs Pritchard quickly. "She's made herself quite useful. I wouldn't want to be without her now. And after all, gentle folks have servants in the house."

Pritchard grunted and carried on eating but his wife hadn't finished. "I seem to remember Adam Trevelyan will be re-applying for his ticket of leave in a few months," she said casually, "such a shame for us because he's been so useful."

Eva, who was filling the kettle, glanced at her and noticed her cheeks had reddened. Mr Pritchard didn't notice his wife's heightened colour but it was obvious to Eva that her mistress liked Adam Trevelyan – although what she saw in him Eva couldn't imagine. If he were to smile, he might indeed be good-looking but much of the time his dark eyes were hooded and he scowled and glowered. During the time she'd been on the farm, Eva had never seen him smile, but then she didn't seek him out like her mistress did. Not that Polly Pritchard often found Adam, for he always seemed to be working on some distant part of Pritchard's land. To give him credit, he worked hard and that was probably why he'd been so useful to Pritchard and had contributed to the success of the farm.

"Don't worry your pretty head about young Trevelyan." Pritchard wiped his mouth with the back of his hand. "He failed to get his ticket the last time and he'll fail this time. The man can't help himself – he's too hot-headed."

"But he's been very calm the last few months."

Pritchard chewed silently for a while. "You may have a point. Don't worry your pretty head. If he doesn't disgrace himself in the next few months and lose his ticket, I'll make sure he does."

"How will you do that?" Mrs Pritchard's tone was innocent, almost as if she wasn't interested, but her expression said otherwise. She fixed her husband with an intense look.

"That's man's business, my dear. Leave it to me. Trevelyan might have quietened down for a while but push him hard enough and he'll snap. He did last time, didn't he?"

Mrs Pritchard frowned. "But that nasty man Turley has gone now. And all the other men seem to treat Trevelyan with respect."

"The men do as I tell 'em."

"D'you mean you arranged for Turley to anger Trevelyan?" she asked in what Eva judged was genuine surprise.

Pritchard nodded, a self-satisfied smile on his face. "Why all the interest in Trevelyan, my dear?"

"Oh, I'm not interested in him at all. It's just that he's been so useful."

Pritchard grunted and carried on eating.

Eva set the kettle on the stove and turned away in case her face should betray her. So, Pritchard had contrived for that sour-faced man to lose his ticket. She shouldn't have been shocked because she'd been present for many other such conversations during the weeks she'd been on the Pritchard's farm, with the master boasting of various petty swindles. But somehow, to cheat a man out of his chance of freedom seemed to be inexcusable. It was so close to home she could identify with Trevelyan's pain. No wonder he never smiled. Although if his temper was as bad as Pritchard had suggested perhaps it hadn't needed much arranging.

Eva cleared the plates away and carried an apple pie to the table.

"But suppose you're right and he loses his ticket for the second time. He might not be so hardworking for another year. Perhaps it would be a good idea to make sure he works closer to the farmhouse. He spends too much time away." Mrs Pritchard's voice was silky-smooth.

"He'll work as hard as I tell him to! Of course, he'll be disappointed at first but we'll give him a sweetener."

"Oh? What did you have in mind?"

He lowered his voice. "A man will settle when he has a woman. I'll let 'im have Anna."

"Eva! Her name's Eva!" Mrs Pritchard's voice was shrill.

"Hush! There's no point telling the girl yet."

Eva was on her way to fetch water and with her back to the table, she was almost out of the door. She forced herself to carry on without faltering or giving the impression she'd overheard Pritchard's comment. There was no doubt the sullen Adam Trevelyan would laugh when offered such a 'sweetener' but suppose he didn't? It wasn't as if Pritchard was offering him a wife – just a woman – someone to use and cast aside. Unless he got his ticket of leave. Then, he'd leave the Pritchard's farm and she wouldn't have to worry.

Later, after she'd tidied away, she strolled to the stables where she knew Trevelyan often spent time with the horses. He hadn't been away from the farm for a week and she suspected the longer he remained close to Pritchard, the more likely it was he'd be trapped into another year of service. Out, mending fences or whatever it was he did when he was away from the farm, he was probably safe but Pritchard hadn't mentioned any such trips.

"Good evening, Mr Trevelyan," she said politely when she found him brushing one of the horses.

He turned abruptly, his face alarmed, although when he saw her, he relaxed. "Good evening, miss. You startled me, I thought you were Mrs Pritchard. Can I help you?"

He turned away and carried on with long sweeps of the brush down the horse's glossy coat.

"No, thank you but I think I can be of help to you."

"Oh?" He stopped brushing and turned towards her; his brows drawn together. "Did your mistress send you?"

"Nobody sent me. In fact, if she knew I was here, she'd be furious... I overheard a conversation earlier between Mr and Mrs Pritchard and..." She hesitated, wondering if he'd believe her.

"Go on..."

"They were discussing your ticket of leave which I understand you should be granted shortly."

"Yes..."

"Well, Mr Pritchard said he'd make sure you failed to get it so you'd have to stay with him another year."

"The hell, he did!"

Eva took a step backwards, shocked at his anger.

"And how does he propose to do that?" Trevelyan asked more gently.

"He said the last time, he'd arranged for a man to provoke you – a man called Turvey or..."

"Turley!" Trevelyan put down the brush and stroked the horse's nose. It seemed to have picked up on his agitation and snorted, his tail swishing and his ears flat.

"Mr Pritchard said he'd do the same thing again," Eva said.

"Like hell, he will!"

Eva backed further away. There was every chance this man would be goaded into losing his temper judging by his reactions to the news and if so, he'd be kept on and Pritchard might carry out his threat to give her to Trevelyan.

She turned to go. "I thought you ought to know."

"Yes, thank you." His voice was controlled and she noticed his hands were now by his side, his shoulders down. "And may I enquire why you'd tell me this?"

She hesitated again, not wanting to let him know her real reason. "I thought you ought to know."

"Really? I can't think why you'd care. Are you sure your mistress hasn't sent you? After all, it's not like I've ever taken an interest in you." He narrowed his eyes and studied her.

"An interest in *me*?" Did he think she was trying to curry favour with him because she liked him?

"I assure you, Mr Trevelyan, that thought had not occurred to me. The truth is, I'm not interested in you in the slightest but if you must know, I also overheard Mr Pritchard say in order to keep you happy once you'd lost your ticket, he would 'sweeten' you up by giving me to you! And it's that possibility I'm trying to avoid!"

Eva expected to see the pinched lips, the narrowed eyes and the bunched fists again, so she was surprised when he burst out laughing. How dare he? She turned on her heel and strode back to the house, her back straight, but her face red with shame. His laughter had revealed exactly what he thought of her.

It was for the best. He'd made it clear he found the prospect of Eva being given to him ludicrous. That was good, she told herself. She didn't like him either. But now he'd been warned of Pritchard's plans, he'd be on his guard and with luck, she wouldn't ever see him again once his ticket of leave had been granted. Nevertheless, hot tears of humiliation stung her eyes and trickled down her cheeks as she walked back to her room.

Oh, Kathleen, you were so right about men.

CHAPTER SEVEN

Adam groaned. He'd hurt the girl's feelings. That hadn't been his intention at all. He was grateful to her for the warning and for letting him know Pritchard had tricked him once. Not, of course, that it was anyone's fault but his. If he'd kept his temper, he wouldn't have ended up in a fight and he'd be working for himself on his own land. Now he knew Pritchard's plans, he'd be very careful. Although, he realised with a sinking heart, even if he behaved perfectly, Pritchard could accuse him of anything and he would lose his ticket anyway. He needed to think. But first, he must thank the girl and beg her pardon. He'd been unforgivably rude.

He waited until the moon had risen, then walked silently to the back of the farmhouse, keeping to the kitchen end of the building. Having mended the roof a few months before, he knew the Pritchards' bedroom was at the other end and suspected the shed-like addition near the kitchen belonged to the girl. Not wanting to frighten her, he stood back from the open window and cleared his throat. When that failed to draw her attention, he called softly, "Hello…"

Rustling came from inside the room and when she pulled the curtain back, she shrieked in surprise.

"Shhh!" he said sharply, stepping closer to the window where the shadows were deeper.

"How dare you come here shouting through my window and then tell me to be quiet!"

"I'm sorry." He lowered his voice, not wanting to anger her further and risk her waking Pritchard. "But I didn't exactly shout."

"Well, what do you want?" She came closer to the window, the soft moonlight falling on her face. She looked very different without the cap she wore during the day. He was surprised her hair was so short. If he'd thought about it at all, he'd have assumed it was pinned up. However, her face was framed by short, dark curls that were lit from behind by the candle in her room, giving her a copper halo.

"If you don't state your business, Mr Trevelyan, I shall scream."

"No, please! I… I ask your forgiveness for the intrusion but I came to thank you and to beg your pardon for my rudeness."

"You could have done that tomorrow morning."

"It's best I keep away from the house… and particularly its mistress. And tomorrow, I leave early for Sydney. I won't be back until late. So, I thought this the best way. I had no intention of frightening you. I wanted to express my appreciation of your warning of Pritchard's intentions and to apologise for my laugher. It may have seemed it was aimed at you but—"

"No need to explain, I understand perfectly." She began to lower the curtain.

"Wait! I wonder if I could do something for you to make up for my poor manners. Perhaps I could bring you something back from Sydney?" he asked, surprising himself at his offer. He certainly hadn't considered such a possibility earlier, when he'd decided to beg her pardon. But then he hadn't considered how she might react at all. Now, he was reluctant to let her go before he'd explained himself even though she didn't seem to want his explanation.

"Thank you, Mr Trevelyan, I have no money to spare for trifles and indeed, there's no need to mention the matter again. In fact, I would prefer it if you didn't. If Mr or Mrs Pritchard learned I'd spoken of their conversation, I would be sure to receive a beating – and I receive enough of those. So, please, there's no need to talk about this again. But I appreciate your offer. Now if that's all, I must retire, I shall be up before sunrise."

"Yes, of course." He nodded politely. "I shall be leaving at first light, so if you think of something you'd like in town, please let me know. I shall, of course, pay. Well, I'll bid you good night."

"Good night."

"No, wait! I almost forgot, I would like to know your name."

"You have no need of my name." She let the curtain drop, then added, quietly, "but it's Eva Bonner."

"Good night, Mistress Eva Bonner."

Seconds later the glow from inside was extinguished and there was the sound of rustling as she climbed on to her straw mattress.

He stood there a few minutes, staring at the shabby, moonlit curtains where a few seconds before, her face, framed by dark curls and a copper halo, had itself been framed by the window, like an oil painting.

"Eva Bonner," he said softly to himself. As he turned and walked back through the moonlight to the hut where the male workers slept, accompanied by the song of the crickets and katydids, the image stayed with him.

Eva rose before dawn, washed quickly and dressed. It had been a stifling night and promised to be a scorching day. The morning sounds of this strange country fascinated Eva but since she'd arrived, she'd had no time to explore the forest. Mrs Pritchard had kept her busy, and had forbidden her to go past the fence around the main farm area. With warnings of strange creatures that feasted on humans, and vicious savages who could become invisible at will, it seemed Mrs Pritchard wanted to frighten her into complying. Eva wondered how the simple fence could keep such dreadful terrors out but when she'd asked, Mrs Pritchard had slapped Eva for her insolence.

From time to time, exotic birds flew up above the tree canopy in flashes of brilliant colours, screeching and squawking, and strange animals could be glimpsed, leaping through the tall grass, or peeping timidly from lofty tree boughs. She observed them with a mixture of fear and enthralment. How different this grey–green landscape was from the bustling streets of London.

Eva wondered what Kathleen was doing now. She was probably only a few miles away in Sydney, working as a farmhand, servant or seamstress. Such bad luck Eva had been taken by Pritchard, but it must be possible to find where Kathleen had gone and even though she could neither read nor write, she might be able to find someone to do both if Eva could get a letter to her.

From overheard conversations at the dinner table, Eva knew Governor Phillip was the man who decided the fate of each convict and she determined to send him a letter to enquire where Kathleen was. There were two problems. First, she didn't know how to get a letter to the governor. Second, even if she could get one to him, would he bother to reply to a convict? It occurred to her if Adam Trevelyan truly wanted to show his gratitude, he might deliver a letter for her while he was in Sydney. As soon as the idea crept into her mind, she dismissed it. Last night, he might have been grateful and rashly offered to bring her something back from town but she doubted he'd meant it. Nobody did a good turn unless it was for gain and how would it profit Trevelyan to spend time going to Government House?

But what did she have to lose by asking? He could either refuse, or agree to deliver it, with no intention of doing so... or, he might just do as she'd asked.

She found him loading boxes on to the cart, and when he saw her, he stopped, wiped his forehead with his kerchief, and smiled at her. How different he was when he wasn't scowling. However, she suspected the smile would be replaced by annoyance when she asked him to deliver her letter.

"I am desperate for news of my sister," Eva said, keeping up the pretence. After all, if he knew Kathleen was simply a friend, he might not try so hard to find her. But to her surprise, Adam continued to smile and he took the letter.

"I'd be glad to deliver it." He tucked it in his pocket.

"Thank you." She turned to go. Was it possible he'd discover where Kathleen had gone? She suppressed her excitement, after all, she might have taken the chance and asked him to do her a favour but he hadn't done it yet. And then, she had an idea. If she'd taken a chance, why shouldn't he?

Eva stopped and turned back to him. "It occurred to me... since you're so close to being granted your ticket, you might ask if it could be awarded a little earlier."

He considered for a second. "But any request I made would have to be supported by Pritchard and we both know that will never happen."

"Why not ask anyway? You could always explain what happened last year. You've nothing to lose..."

"Yes, I suppose I could ask someone in the governor's office."

"Eva? Where are you?" It was Mrs Pritchard, shouting from the house, her voice shrill and demanding.

"Good luck," she said, an anxious look on her face, and holding her cap to her head she fled to the house, risking a glance over her shoulder to see him still watching her. He patted his pocket and nodded as if to tell her he would deliver her letter.

CHAPTER EIGHT

Adam was in Sydney Town and in no hurry to return to Pritchard's farm. He'd concluded his business quickly and made his way to the back of the two-storey Government House – the grandest building in Sydney. It was where the government offices were situated and Adam handed in Eva's letter to the clerk. The short, tubby man adjusted his spectacles and consulted one of the many ledgers on the shelf behind his desk.

"Kathleen O'Marne? Arrived on the *Lady Amelia*?" He craned his neck to look at Eva's letter again. "Hmm. I'm afraid that particular convict died shortly after being sent to work on a farm on the other side of Sydney. Cause of death... Hmm, it appears to be heat exhaustion exacerbated by pre-existing illness." He looked up at Adam. "Probably ill when she arrived. It's a common story." He took off his glasses and closing the ledger, he put it back on the shelf. "Was there something else?"

Adam said he'd also like to enquire whether his ticket might be brought forward by a few weeks and explained he had reason to believe his master intended to make false accusations to prevent him from receiving it.

"Hmm," the clerk said and put his spectacles back on. "It's a common story. I'll let Governor Phillips know. He's a fair man and he won't stand for any nonsense. Let me just make a few notes." He scribbled in his book. "Now, when will you be back?"

"Tuesday."

"I'll see if I can find out anything for you by then."

Adam left the grounds with a feeling of optimism. The clerk hadn't promised he'd be able to help but at least he'd listened and had promised to put his case to the governor. But his happiness was tinged with sadness for Eva, whose sister had died. She smiled so rarely and when he returned, he was going to make her cry again.

How cruel life was. Handing out favour to some and punishment to others, seemingly on a whim. Although, he warned himself, he didn't have the ticket in his hand yet. If Pritchard heard about Adam's accusation he'd simply contradict it and if the governor upheld Pritchard's claim and Adam had to return to the farm for a further year, life would be unbearable.

Would Pritchard's 'sweetener' still be on offer? A face framed by a window with a copper halo filled his thoughts. Eva. Given to him as compensation for his lack of freedom. He'd never use her but the prospect of spending more time with her was appealing. More than appealing... Stop! He must not be distracted from his plans, and anyway why would Pritchard want to sweeten him up? Indeed, he'd probably try to make Adam's life hell.

He patted his pocket and checked the lacy handkerchief he'd bought Eva was still there.

"For a special lady?" the shopkeeper had asked conversationally when he'd bought it earlier.

"No. No one special."

Well, she wasn't special – not to him. He simply felt sorry for a girl who'd lost her sister and didn't yet know it.

It suddenly occurred to him that for a girl who wasn't special to him, he'd spent much of the day thinking about Eva Bonner.

It would stop.

Hadn't he sworn to be single-minded about his plans to return to England? He'd no doubt he'd be accepted back into Cornish society; he'd received letters of support from family friends who, like many Cornishmen, didn't consider smuggling a crime. Everyone knew the dubious circumstances under which Adam had been condemned.

Once he had his ticket, he'd work all hours until he'd added sufficient money to the small sum he'd already earned. And when he'd been granted his pardon, he'd return home and his family would live in comfort. His plans were simple. They were as good as written in stone.

News from Cornwall was that Mr Pengelly was setting his sights too high and after several failed attempts, Rosenwyn had still not made the match that would launch the Pengellys into society. Adam dreamed of demonstrating he was more than worthy of her hand. But he no longer desired her. Ironically, her father had been responsible for sending him to Sydney – a place that had more opportunities to make a fortune than he'd have been offered in Cornwall. Not yet of course, but once he was free...

Adam wouldn't return to England until he was a wealthy man. A wealthy Trevelyan. A man Mr Pengelly would want for his daughter but now could never acquire. Adam's dream was possible, and nothing and no one was going to get in his way.

While he'd been in Sydney, Adam had visited Mr Bartholomew Shaw, a former convict, who was now in the packet trade along the Parramatta River. Mr Shaw was thinking of retiring. He wanted someone younger to sail his sloop, the *May Queen*, for him, as a partner to begin with, then with a view to buying him out. Adam was an excellent sailor and he impressed Mr Shaw who offered him the partnership, saying he'd wait until Adam got his ticket. But he made it clear if Adam didn't get it soon, he'd find someone else as he was keen to get on with his own plans.

This opportunity would put Adam one step closer to returning home. Success was within reach so long as he kept on the right side of Pritchard. So, why wasn't he elated? Why didn't he feel the satisfaction he'd expected to feel? Why couldn't he imagine his feet planted squarely on the heaving deck, the wind blowing through his hair and filling the sails of the *May Queen*? Enjoying the freedom of the open sea? He knew why. It was because his mind was filled with images of Eva. Last night she'd smiled. Tonight, her heart would break. And he would be the one to give her the tragic news.

By the time he'd arrived home, settled the horse, and eaten a meal, it was dark. The moon was almost full in the clear sky and it cast sufficient silver light for him to take the same route as the previous night and to call gently at her window – keeping a respectful distance away.

Instantly the curtain was pulled aside. Her smile was one of relief and welcome.

"Did you find Kathleen?" Her voice was eager, excited.

He took a deep breath, readying himself to break the bad news but before he could stop, he heard himself say, "No. I must enquire when I return, the clerk says he should know by then."

What had he been thinking? He held his breath. Surely, she could see he'd lied?

But no. She gasped with delight and her eyes lit up with the thought she might know by the following week. "How can I thank you?"

What could he say? He stared at her for a second and then remembered the handkerchief. "This is for you."

Her face softened and she'd smiled as she took the gift.

Then, he'd been glad of his lie.

Let her have a week of relative happiness. After all, there was nothing she could do about her sister now.

Each night after darkness had fallen and the Pritchards had gone to bed, Eva waited eagerly for Adam to visit. It had become the best part of her day. He still initially maintained a respectful distance but as the night wore on, he drew closer to the window, ostensibly so they could hear each other's whispers and he could hide in the shadow of the wall. With their heads together in the dark, she breathed in the smell of soap that accompanied him, and was touched that after a hard, dusty and hot day at work, he bothered to wash before he came to see her. She couldn't imagine any of the other men on the farm, including Mr Pritchard bothering to do that for a woman.

The following Tuesday, Adam left early in the morning for Sydney with a cart of produce from the farm and a list of goods to buy. Eva knew he also intended to visit Government House to find out about his early application for a ticket as well as to ask for news about Kathleen. However, he'd returned late and she'd worried he wouldn't come to tell her how the visit had gone. When she heard his polite cough outside the window and his call, she'd instantly drawn back the curtains. He was standing further off than usual. Heavy clouds rolled across the sky, concealing the moon and hiding his face in deep shadow.

"Have you any news about your ticket?" she whispered.

He hesitated but finally said, "Yes, the governor's agreed to look on my request with favour and he'll let me know soon."

"That is such good news!" She gripped the window frame and leaned towards him. Why was he keeping his distance?

"Yes, but..." His voice was strained. Not like when he usually came to her at night.

The shadows hid his features but she could see he was looking down at the ground.

"Kathleen?" she asked. Something was wrong. "Do you know where she is?"

"Yes." He spoke slowly. "That is, I found out—"

"Where is she? How is she?" Eva frowned. Why didn't he tell her?

Adam looked up and as the clouds slid away from the moon, she saw the light reflected in his eyes. They seemed brighter than usual.

"She's well and she's in the women's camp but she will leave for Norfolk Island, Wednesday sennight."

"Norfolk Island? But that's miles from Sydney." Eva had heard of the penal colony that the governor had set up in the middle of the ocean. It was so far away, Kathleen might as well be about to set sail for England.

"The governor asked for volunteers to live there and your sister agreed to go."

Why was Adam behaving so strangely? It was as if he didn't want to tell her.

"Kathleen volunteered?"

He nodded.

A great weight seemed to squeeze her chest, pressing the air out of her. Why had Kathleen volunteered to go to a strange island so far away? How would they ever see each other again?

Eva pushed the words past the painful lump in her throat. "Thank you, Adam, that was very kind of you to find out for me. I can't pretend I'm not disappointed but it's not as though I'm free to see her now, so it hardly matters she's going somewhere else. But at least she's well. Please may I ask one more favour? Would you take a letter to her, for me?"

Adam hesitated, then agreed. He bade her goodnight and left shortly after.

Eva cried herself to sleep. She told herself she was sad because she wouldn't see Kathleen again. Even the assurance that her friend was well didn't console her. But somewhere deep down, Eva knew she was crying for something that she and Adam had shared but that now had gone.

CHAPTER NINE

Adam had lied to Eva again. But at least that night she hadn't been mourning the death of her sister. The ship leaving for Norfolk Island would set sail in eight days, and by the time Eva discovered the truth, many years would have passed. During that time, Kathleen could well have died. Indeed, either he or Eva could be dead in this harsh uncompromising climate. He'd promised to take a letter to Kathleen the following week, so more lies would be necessary. But he'd done it twice to save her pain. What difference would once more make?

He went back to her window the next night. He hadn't seen her all day and he wondered how she was coping with the unwelcome news that she wouldn't see her sister again. More than that, he simply wanted to see her. He wanted to be near her. To hear her voice. To see her smile. To breathe in the scent of her.

Thunder boomed in the distance, and Adam stepped nearer to the window, his face close to hers so they could whisper yet still hear each other above the rumbling. He was describing a kangaroo he'd seen earlier, with a baby in her pocket, when he turned slightly, and his lips accidentally touched Eva's cheek. At the instant he realised what had happened, he expected her to step away, perhaps to raise her hand to her cheek or even to slap him, but she didn't move and neither, he realised, had he. Their faces were so close he could feel her warmth and hear her stifled gasp. Without thinking, he leaned forwards once again to kiss her but she'd turned towards him, and instead of finding the softness of her cheek, he brushed his lips across the corner of hers. Then, with a finger on her chin, he turned her face so his lips covered hers completely. She trembled but didn't pull away. He placed his hand on the back of her head and allowed his fingers to extend into her curls and to hold her firmly against him as their kiss became more passionate.

An animal howled somewhere in the bush, making them both jump apart and, in that instant, he realised he'd made a grave mistake. Not only had he already deceived her but he was prepared to do it again next week when he told her he'd given the letter to Kathleen. And worse, he would soon be leaving the farm, abandoning her. He had no right to play with her affections. And anyway, hadn't he promised himself he wouldn't let anything stand in the way of his plans to return to his family? Hadn't he vowed to show Hugh Pengelly he'd triumphed over adversity? And if he was honest, didn't he want Rosenwyn to see what she'd lost?

He stepped backwards, away from her. "I'm sorry. I shouldn't have done that. Please accept my apologies."

Her mouth open in shock as if he'd struck her, and he looked away. He couldn't bear to see the pain in her eyes. Turning he walked quickly into the darkness. How could he have been so thoughtless? *Fool. Fool.*

As he walked silently through the night, the taste and sensation of her kiss were still on his lips, and he angrily wiped his sleeve across his mouth.

Stupid. Cruel. He cursed himself for his heartless lack of self-restraint.

Eva stood at the window watching Adam melt into the shadows. Why had he apologised for kissing her? True, it had begun accidentally, but it was he who'd turned her face towards him. Had he been shocked she hadn't stopped him? Why? Why?

Eva was hurt but not surprised. She'd begun to think he liked her – after all, didn't the gift of the handkerchief demonstrate that and his appearances each night? But it appeared she'd misunderstood.

Well, she knew now. Soon, he'd have his ticket of leave and be gone and there'd be no further embarrassment. She was better off keeping herself to herself. She thought of Kathleen and how disappointed she'd be. Why couldn't she ever learn? Midshipman Jeremy Findlay. Now Adam Trevalyan.

In future, she'd work hard until she, too, was granted a ticket and then she'd leave the Pritchards' and go to Sydney. There, she'd work as a seamstress or perhaps she'd offer reading and writing services for those who didn't know their letters. She'd earn her own money and be independent. Alone.

But as much as Eva wanted to avoid Adam, she had a problem. The letter to Kathleen was ready and she'd have to hand it to him in person or risk it not being delivered. On several occasions during the next few days, she walked to the stable looking for him while on errands and even risked the ribald comments of the other men by taking a detour near the men's hut. But he was nowhere to be found.

However, before sunrise on the morning Adam was due to go to Sydney, he came past the kitchen. He was polite but distant. Waiting at the door to keep an eye out for Mrs Pritchard, he enquired if Eva had the letter. It was in her pocket and when she handed it over, he courteously nodded and was gone. Just like a stranger.

That night she'd gone to bed not expecting him to visit but to her delight, she heard him cough gently and call out. She sprang out of bed and pulled the curtain aside. Adam stepped back, cleared his throat and said, "I gave the letter to your sister." He nodded politely and turned to go.

"Please, wait! How was she?" Eva was so desperate for news of Kathleen that it was worth risking Adam's annoyance.

"She's well." He paused but did not make eye contact. "She read your letter and asked me to thank you and tell you it will be difficult to send letters back from Norfolk Island but she'll try. And... and, she sent her love."

Eva stared at him in silence.

"I wanted to thank you for suggesting I apply for my ticket. Apparently, the governor will look favourably on my request and I'll receive it early." Adam turned and was gone.

Eva stared into the darkness wondering if she'd misheard. No, there was no doubt. He'd definitely said Kathleen had read the letter and would try to reply and she'd also sent Eva her love.

There was only one explanation. Adam was lying. Kathleen could neither read nor write. Eva had offered to teach her during the long hours on the *Lady Amelia* but Kathleen had scoffed and asked what good it would do her. "I can sew, dig, cook and wash clothes. That's all that'll be asked of me in Sydney."

When Eva had sent her letter, she'd assumed Kathleen would take it away and ask someone to read it to her – perhaps even Adam, but he hadn't mentioned reading it to her. And Kathleen would never have sent her love. Not like a real sister. She'd saved her love for Aoife.

So, why had Adam lied?

There was a bitter taste in her mouth. She'd trusted him but he was like everyone else – simply interested in themselves. No, not like everyone else. He was worse. At least the Pritchards made it obvious they were greedy and self-serving. Adam had pretended to be a friend.

CHAPTER TEN

Eva was sweeping the kitchen floor early one morning when she heard men's voices outside. She wondered if some of the farmhands were arguing, and briefly hoped Adam wasn't involved. Surely, he wouldn't be so foolish as to jeopardise his chance of freedom again? But what would she know? It seemed she didn't know him at all.

Eva leaned the broom against the wall and peered through the back door as the shouts became angrier. With a sinking heart, she recognised the voices. One of them was Adam. And, of all people, the other was Mr Pritchard.

It was still dark with only the merest suggestion of light in the eastern sky. The furious voices were coming from near the barn and she wondered whether her appearance might stop a fight before it began or would she put herself in danger of a beating later? As she hesitated, Mr Pritchard moaned loudly and there was a thud as something hit the ground.

Then silence.

Eva ran to the barn where she found Adam crouching next to Mr Pritchard with his hands on the motionless man's neck.

"Adam!" Eva's hands flew to her mouth. Had he killed the master? No, that wasn't possible.

He looked up and in the pale dawn light, she could see his face, white with shock. It wasn't the face of a murderer.

"Eva! Mr Pritchard collapsed. I can't feel a pulse. Please call his wife and I'll ride for the doctor."

No, whatever Eva thought about Adam, she truly believed this had been a tragic accident.

Mrs Pritchard, roused by the shouting, appeared, her eyes wide in horror. "What have you done? Take your hands off him!"

She yelled for one of the farmhands to ride for Dr Wilson and a constable. Then, kneeling in the dust, she cradled her husband's head, rocking back and forth.

"I knew you had a temper, but murder...?" Her face twisted with fury and she fixed Adam with a cold, hard stare.

"No! Mrs Pritchard, I swear, I didn't touch him. I showed him my ticket of leave and he threatened me but please believe me, I didn't lay a hand on him. He collapsed."

"Liar!"

"Please! I give you my word. Master clutched his heart and—"

"Enough! Let's see what the constable says. With your history, I wouldn't be surprised if you don't swing for this! It's your word against mine and I know who people will believe!"

Vindictive Mrs Pritchard was likely to carry out her threat. Eva felt sick. If it hadn't been for her suggesting Adam apply for his ticket early, this would never have happened. But if Adam had a witness... She stepped forward and in a trembling voice, she said, "Please, Mistress, Adam didn't touch your husband. I was here and I saw it all. Mr Pritchard clutched his heart and fell, just as Adam said."

Would Mrs Pritchard believe her?

"How convenient!" Mrs Pritchard's lip curled in scorn. "What would you have been doing out here?"

"I was with Adam. We were together when he showed Mr Pritchard his ticket."

Adam stared at Eva his eyes wide in shock.

"Together? How could you have been together? How did you know he had his ticket?" Mrs Pritchard's jaw dropped, then her face twisted with distaste. She stood, leaving her husband lying on the ground. "So, you and Adam...? I don't believe it... Were the two of you carrying on right under my nose?"

Adam looked at Eva. Eva looked at her feet. What had she done? She'd lied to save Adam. What had she been thinking? But how could that be wrong? Adam was innocent. And Eva knew her mistress would lash out at anyone when she was troubled. Who better to hurt than the man who'd rejected her advances?

"You whore!" Mrs Pritchard sprang at Eva and slapped her.

The doctor arrived and after examining Mr Pritchard, he proclaimed him dead.

"I understand you've called for a constable. I'll stay until he arrives but it seems certain your husband suffered a paroxysm of the heart. I've been treating him for a cardiac condition for some time and I'd warned him not to exert himself unduly. It appears he disregarded my advice. Now, madam, I understand your distress and your wish to apportion blame but I doubt this is a police matter. I've looked closely and there's no bruising or sign of a fight, so I'd strongly urge you to throw your energy into considering your future and not worrying about bringing charges. I'm convinced there was no foul play involved here."

When the doctor and constable had gone, Mrs Pritchard turned to Adam. "Get off my land." Her words were slow and deliberate. "You have your ticket, so go! And take *her* with you!" She pointed at Eva. "I'll take the money from what my husband owed you to cover the loss of two servants. Now get off my property!'"

It had been a moment of madness in claiming she'd been with Adam when he'd handed the ticket to Mr Pritchard. Eva hadn't intended to give the impression she and Adam had been 'carrying on' as Mrs Pritchard had claimed, and she'd been so surprised at the accusation, she'd been speechless. It seemed Adam had been so shocked, he hadn't found the words to deny it either.

How ironic. Adam hadn't even needed an alibi. The doctor had been convinced he hadn't been involved and he'd persuaded the constable it had been an accident. And now, Eva had ruined her reputation for nothing.

Mrs Pritchard was not a woman to show mercy. She'd lost her husband – not that she'd loved him but he'd provided a good life for her. In addition, she'd lost the man she'd taken a fancy to, as well as believing he'd been having a love affair with the servant she held in contempt.

Any joy Eva might have felt at escaping from the Pritchard's farm was overwhelmed by the sinking feeling in her stomach. She'd inadvertently created a disaster for Adam. He'd been relying on the money he was owed by Pritchard to set up a business. Now instead of a sum of money, Adam had a servant he didn't want.

Why hadn't she kept quiet? After all, Adam was nothing to her.

Now, both on the back of the horse on which Adam had planned to travel into Sydney on his own, his body was pressed against her rigid back. At the beginning of the journey, she'd suggested he pass her on to somebody else and recoup the money as soon as they arrived in Sydney.

"I wouldn't get anywhere near the full amount for you." His tone was bitter. "Mrs Pritchard wanted to exact her revenge on both of us – me for rejecting her advances and you because you led her to believe you'd tempted me away. And she certainly made me pay for it."

After that, they'd both remained silent and Eva took the opportunity to study the landscape. Her journey to Pritchard's farm had been viewed through tear-filled eyes, having been pulled from Kathleen's side, and she'd not taken much in. Now, she peered into the tangled depths of the grey-green forests that flanked the road. When the woods gave way to open land, she watched kangaroos bounding through the long grass. Such a wondrous place. She had the urge to slip off the horse and to run and run – escape from Adam and from all the problems she'd caused. But where would she go? This country with its harsh climate and conditions was indeed a prison with miles of inhospitable terrain, instead of walls.

When they reached Sydney, they dismounted outside the George Inn. Adam summoned the boy who led the horse to the stable and then beckoned to Eva to follow the innkeeper upstairs.

"I can't afford two rooms," he said when the innkeeper had gone, "so we'll just have to manage until I can find you a new place." The room was small with a narrow bed, scratched and battered furniture and a window which looked out over the noisy street. "Take the bed. I won't be back until late."

He left shortly after and with her nose to a dirty pane of glass in the window, she watched him turn right and walk along the street, his head bowed and shoulders hunched. On the journey, Eva had made up her mind to find Kathleen and to see what she'd advise. It was unlikely Adam would ever forgive her so she must find a way of paying him back and freeing herself from him. The more she thought about it, the angrier she became. It had been her intention to help him. He was behaving as if she'd deliberately ruined everything. Well, she'd put it right. She'd ask the innkeeper to direct her to Government House to find out where Kathleen was, and now, while Adam was out, would be the perfect time to go. She slipped out of the room, but halfway down the stairs, she met Adam coming up.

He frowned in surprise. "Where are you going?"

"I've had enough of you and your silence. I know you're angry with me but I was trying to help you. Now I'm going to find Kathleen." She locked eyes with him, daring him to stop her.

"But..."

Eva put her hands on her hips. "Yes, I know you told me she was on a ship which left for Norfolk Island but I don't believe you. I don't think you found her. I don't think you looked for her at all."

Behind them, a man cleared his throat and made it clear he wanted to go upstairs. Adam gestured to Eva to go to their room.

"I don't believe you gave Kathleen my letter!" she said once he'd closed the door.

"Why would I lie?" His voice was unsteady as if he was hiding something.

"I don't know. Perhaps you'd like to tell me. But you told me that when you gave her the letter, she read it and then she'd write to me when she could. And that she sent me her love."

Adam stared at her silently.

"Kathleen can neither read nor write. And she's not my sister, so I

94

doubt she'd have sent me her love."

"What kind of trickery is this? You told me at length about growing up with your sister! If anyone has lied, it's you!"

"The girl I told you about was Kezzie. She is my sister and she's still in London. Kathleen was a friend who looked after me. We called each other sister because we thought it would increase our chances of being kept together."

"When you said Kezzie, I thought it was your nickname for Kathleen."

"That's no explanation! You deliberately deceived me. You could've told me you didn't have time or even the inclination to look for her but instead, you lied to me! Now I'm going to find out where she is and see if I can be with her. Don't worry, I'll work hard and one day I'll pay you back every single penny, but in the meantime please move aside."

He was standing in the doorway and as she tried to barge past him, he held up a hand to stop her. "Please stay while I explain...You're right. I lied, but it's not as you think. I wanted to find her for you and I did try, but I discovered..." He paused, swallowed and then continued, "I'm afraid Kathleen died a short while ago of heat exhaustion while she was working in the fields... I'm so sorry."

The colour drained from Eva's face and she held her hand to her mouth as if to stifle a scream but no sound came. Could yet another person have been taken from her? What sort of world was this where everyone she became close to was snatched away?

"Why didn't you tell me?" Her voice was small, empty.

"Because I couldn't bear to see the pain in your eyes. It seems to me you've cried too many tears. I know it was wrong but I wanted to spare you for a while."

Eva didn't move, her face a mask of disbelief and shock.

"Eva?" He stepped towards her, enveloping her in his arms. She clung to him sobbing.

Chapter Eleven

Each Friday morning, Eva tipped the money out of the tobacco tin onto the table and after counting it, she paid Mrs Roper, her landlady, for the rooms Adam had rented. Then, she put a small amount aside for the following week's expenses and added the rest to a small wooden, tea box, which grew heavier week by week. The sum in the box was for Adam, should he ever come home and claim it.

Home. It was her home. But not Adam's. He'd made it clear he didn't consider the rooms he rented in Mrs Roper's house his home. And since he'd secured the rooms and agreed on a price with the landlady, he'd only visited a few times.

Mrs Roper, who made it her business to know everybody else's business, reported that *Shaw and Trevelyan's* boat, the *May Queen*, was one of the most successful vessels that traded out of Sydney. This was apparently because of its master, Adam Trevelyan. He set sail whatever the weather or the tide, and his name was trusted beyond all others to collect and deliver goods when others feared to venture out of the harbour. So, Eva knew he'd succeeded in becoming Mr Shaw's partner and in building up a fine reputation.

She wished him well. And one day, she'd pay him back for the inconvenience she'd caused him – with interest. Adam sent her the rent each week, but other than the first two weeks, she hadn't had to touch that money. She paid what she owed Mrs Roper, out of her earnings as a teacher and from the private work she carried out, reading and writing letters for people.

Eva didn't like Fridays. It was the one day of the week when she had to think of Adam. She'd rather have put him completely out of her mind but if the sum she'd amassed in the tea box, and the money he'd earned, was sufficient for him to return to England, then it was best he knew. Once he'd gone, she wouldn't have to think of him ever again.

A few days before, he'd left a message with Mrs Roper to tell Eva he'd arranged for her ticket of leave to be granted shortly. That would mean she'd be able to carry on working in the school and with her private clients until she'd served her sentence. Then she'd return to England and look for Keziah and Henry. She'd written to several of the workhouses in London, including St Margaret's and, so far, no one had replied, but it would be easier to find them when she was there in person.

Now, she must reply to Adam to thank him for arranging her ticket and to let him know about the money she could repay. That would mean meeting him. Whereas Mrs Roper would be happy to locate Adam and pass on a message, Eva didn't trust the landlady with the money. She'd once run a bawdy house in Covent Garden – nothing as grand as Mrs Jenner's establishment, but she'd proudly told Eva her house had been clean and the girls had been happy. Her speciality had been picking pockets, a skill she'd used on one particular gentleman who'd been relieved of his watch and twenty guineas. It transpired he was a Member of Parliament and having called the constables, he demanded an example be made of her. That had resulted in arrest and subsequent transportation to New South Wales on one of the first ships to arrive in Sydney Cove.

Eva was glad of Mrs Roper's friendship but she worried that the light-fingered woman wouldn't be able to resist dipping into the money if she got the opportunity.

Each Friday, Mrs Roper called for the rent and Eva always invited her in for tea. Both women had come to enjoy this weekly ritual, and they spent the time reminiscing about their lives in London.

Eva had told her about Henry and Keziah, and their father's watchmaking business in Black Swan Lane. Mrs Roper had told Eva about her girls and the house she'd rented in Covent Garden. But somehow, the landlady always seemed to turn the conversation to Mr Trevelyan – or 'your nice, young gentleman', as she described him, even though Eva had repeatedly pointed out Adam was definitely not hers.

"You're not trying hard enough, dearie," Mrs Roper said. "Leave it to me. I could put yer hair up and paint yer face a treat. 'E wouldn't be able to leave you alone."

Eva had explained that was the last thing she wanted.

"If I didn't know better, I'd say you was afeared..."

"Nonsense!"

"I know a bad 'un when I see one. And your nice, young gentleman ain't one. There definitely ain't no need to be afeared o' that man."

"I'm not afraid of him... He's pleasant enough but I care nothing for him."

Mrs Roper merely raised her eyebrows and sipped her tea.

"I care nothing for him," she'd told Mrs Roper. It was true. The day they'd first arrived at the George Inn, Adam had once again been tender towards her like he had when they'd kissed through the window of her lean-to on the Pritchard's farm. Then, just as before, he'd inexplicably turned cold.

It would be the last time.

She now felt nothing for him. When he'd confessed he'd kept Kathleen's death from her, she'd been furious until he'd explained he'd wanted to shield her from the grief. She'd believed him and he'd comforted her as she'd cried. Later, she'd surprised herself by showing her forgiveness by kissing him on the cheek and he'd slipped an arm around her waist, then placing a fingertip beneath her chin, he'd tilted her head towards him, as he'd done once before, and gently brushed his lips against hers. He'd drawn back to gauge her reaction but she hadn't pulled away; in fact, she'd demonstrated her consent, by pressing her mouth softly against his. The world had then receded; the sounds from the street, and downstairs in the taproom, all faded and Eva could have been floating on air, her body so tightly pressed against Adam's, she almost felt part of him. He'd lifted her, and she'd wrapped her arms around his neck, nuzzling him as he carried her to the bed.

Suddenly, he'd stopped. And at a signal she hadn't perceived, everything had changed. Adam had paused as if waking from a dream and had lowered her feet to the ground. Mumbling an apology, he'd put on his jacket and hat and had left the room. He hadn't returned until after dark, when he'd crept into the room on unsteady feet, reeking of rum.

He'd folded his jacket as a pillow and had lain down on the floor but she'd whispered through the darkness that being smaller, she could sleep on the chair and he should take the bed because he'd paid for the room.

"Or we could share the bed," Eva had said. That only seemed fair. He'd made it clear he had no interest in her. They'd simply sleep. Eva had lain there the rest of the night, her body rigid, facing away from him.

Somehow, he could turn his emotions on and off – one moment seeming to desire her and the next rejecting her. But she'd still burned for him. Sleep was impossible with him only inches away and if he'd held out his hand to her, she'd have fallen into his arms and given herself to him.

But he hadn't.

She knew he hadn't slept either.

During the small hours, she must have dozed off because it was as if Kathleen was there, "Mavourneen! What were you thinking? He's the same as the others, he'll use you and then when it suits, he'll desert you." The dream had been so real; Eva had sat up and reached out, only to find an empty room.

Adam had half-turned but she'd pretended she'd wanted a drink and had poured herself some ale from the jug, then climbed back into bed,

98

keeping to the edge.

By the time the first rays of the sun tumbled into the room, Kathleen had cooled her ardour and she'd persuaded herself Adam's rejection had been for the best.

CHAPTER TWELVE

Mrs Roper had given things a great deal of thought.

Interesting. Like a candle flame flaring and then immediately being snuffed out. That initial blaze in Eva's eyes when Adam's name was mentioned was immediately quenched. Mrs Roper had spotted that same flash which was immediately extinguished in Adam's eyes on the rare occasions when he came to her house and his gaze had alighted on Eva.

Yes, very interesting.

But had the spark gone? That was the question. Without fanning and coaxing, it would simply fade and die.

Mrs Roper found out when the *May Queen* would arrive in Sydney and had nonchalantly sauntered past just as Adam was bringing the last item of cargo ashore. Perfect timing to greet him and ask about his last trip. She informed him Eva was well and enquired whether he intended to spend time in the rooms he was renting while he was in Sydney.

Adam said he'd be leaving again on another trip in a few days so he'd take a room in the local inn.

Mrs Roper had noticed a momentary glimmer in his eyes at the mention of the girl's name and just as quickly, it had died. What was the matter with them? Why couldn't they see they belonged together? In her profession, she'd learned to differentiate between feigned and real attraction. And if they were still in doubt, they had to look no further than the Bible. Adam and Eva. The first couple in the Bible. How much more obvious was it they were meant for each other? But how could she make them realise?

"Do I owe you any rent?" Adam looked at her anxiously.

Inadvertently, he'd given her an opportunity to arrange a meeting.

"I believe that's something you need to ask Eva." Mrs Roper knew Adam wasn't aware that Eva was paying the rent out of her own earnings. If she appeared uncertain, Adam might decide to visit to find out. "I understand you gave Eva a sum of money, but..." she shrugged and left the sentence hanging.

Adam frowned and she quickly added, "However, if you'd like to visit and find out, Eva and I take tea on a Friday morning when the rent is due, perhaps you'd join us?"

"I can pay you anything outstanding now..."

"It's best you sort it out with Eva."

Well, I shan't delay you longer. I know you're a busy man. Until Friday..." She turned on her heel before he could refuse to visit.

She'd done her best. But suppose he didn't come despite her efforts? Well, she'd simply have to try harder. Adam and Eva deserved their own time in life's Garden of Eden and if their guardian angels hadn't managed to bring them together yet, then she'd simply have to lend a hand.

Bartholomew Shaw arrived as Mrs Roper was leaving.

"How do you know Mrs Roper?" He smiled knowingly at Adam.

"She's my landlady. Why?"

"Landlady, eh? Well, it must be a lively house!"

"Not that I know of. When I'm ashore, I stay at the George Inn. Why should the house be lively?"

"Hannah Roper used to run a well-known bawdy house in Covent Garden," Bartholomew said, slapping Adam on the back, "don't tell me you didn't know?"

"But everything seemed respectable when I looked at the rooms." Adam frowned. Surely Bartholomew had mistaken the woman.

"P'raps she's reformed then." Bartholomew laughed heartily.

Despite telling Mrs Roper he'd visit on Friday, he hadn't intended to stay, merely take the money, hand it to Eva and then make his excuses. But perhaps he needed to spend some time there. He couldn't leave Eva in a brothel. He was sure the house had been respectable when he'd first rented the rooms but much could have changed since then. He'd go and find out. It wouldn't hurt to satisfy himself Eva was well too. Mrs Roper had been vague. Yes, he'd see if Eva was well – nothing more.

Bartholomew Shaw wanted to discuss a new client on Friday morning and Adam didn't get to Mrs Roper's house until after midday. She waved his apology away with a gesture of her hand and directed him to the rooms he rented at the back of the house – the rooms where Eva lived. If he hadn't known better, he'd have thought he saw a look of relief on Mrs Roper's face. Why would she be relieved to see him? Perhaps he'd misread it. Could it have been guilt? He listened intently for voices or signs of any other lodgers or visitors, but all was quiet. If Mrs Roper was running a disorderly house, it was a very *orderly* disorderly house.

Eva's shocked expression suggested the landlady hadn't mentioned the possibility of Adam visiting. He apologised for arriving late, asked how she was and how much he needed to give her for the rent but to his surprise, rather than taking the money, Eva invited him in. She brewed sweet sarsaparilla tea, explaining she was making use of native leaves and hadn't wasted the money he'd given her on expensive black tea. After she'd put the cup in front of him, she placed a wooden tea box on the table and removed the lid.

"This is what I've saved, it's all yours," she said proudly, "I had to use some of the money you gave me for the rent during the first few weeks but now I have a job and I can pay the rent and put something aside to repay you."

"How have you earned so much money?" The box contained a surprisingly large pile of coins.

"I teach in a school on several days a week and I also have a few clients of my own."

"To have made so much in such a short time, you must've worked very hard." His eyes narrowed as he regarded the contents of the tea box. Surely Mrs Roper hadn't recruited Eva?

"I do work hard but I like what I do so it's a labour of love."

"And what exactly is it that you do?" He kept his voice casual.

"So many questions." She tilted her head to one side and pursed her lips. "I wonder that you're interested in what I do with my time."

"Just making conversation." Why had her expression suddenly become guarded?

Since he'd last seen her, the hollows in her cheeks had filled out and her hair was now long enough to pin up in a style that softly framed her face. She was beautiful. He realised he was staring at her. He forced himself to look away, hiding his embarrassment with stories of his journeys on the *May Queen*.

As he finished his tea and prepared to leave, he wondered if it wouldn't be better to stay in his room in Mrs Roper's house rather than find lodgings in the George Inn. A ship from England had arrived in Sydney shortly after the *May Queen* had moored and by now, the inn would probably be full. It would only be for a few days. Just until his next trip and he could keep an eye on Eva and make sure Mrs Roper wasn't exploiting her.

How Eva earns her money has nothing to do with you, he told himself, *leave it be. She seems happy and safe.*

But it wasn't sensible to spend money on lodgings when he had a room here.

Eva, however, pressed her lips together in a slight grimace when he announced his intention to sleep in his room for a few nights.

She blushed as she said, "I have a client coming in half an hour. I wonder if it would be possible for you to stay in your room, please? Mr Connor's rather sensitive about coming to see me and I wouldn't want him upset. I hope that doesn't inconvenience you. If you intend to stay more often, I'll ensure he comes when you're out."

"Of course. I shall stay in my room."

Why had she avoided telling him what she did with her clients? Respectable women didn't spend time alone with men. But perhaps she wouldn't be alone. Yes, that was it; the man was bringing a child for a lesson. But why would a man be so sensitive about coming to Eva? Adam's thoughts whirled.

Shortly after, there was a knock at the door. Adam strained to hear what was going on, listening for a child's voice but there was definitely only one visitor – a man with what Adam thought was a ridiculously high-pitched voice, and a laugh that grated on his nerves.

What was Eva doing? Why hadn't he simply demanded she explain what she did before Mr Connor had arrived? She'd obviously been reluctant to tell him.

You have no claim on her. So long as she pays you back, she can behave as she wishes.

But still, he wondered, what was she doing and why did the man keep laughing?

The kettle sang on the stove and sounds of tea-making came through the door but other than that, no one spoke. Then the rattle of cup against saucer was accompanied by conversation although Adam couldn't hear what they were saying and shortly after, there was only murmuring, until Eva said quite clearly, "Good, but that's not quite right. Just a little more pressure. Yes, good."

Seconds later, Eva squealed, and Connor exclaimed, "Oh! Oh!" and then, cups rattled, the table moved and chairs scraped.

What were they doing? His hand went to the doorknob but he forced himself to stop before he turned it. He pressed his forehead to the door, willing his heart to stop hammering.

It had been such a mistake to come. He'd tried so hard to keep her from his mind but now with thoughts of other men enjoying her company. Possibly enjoying more than simply her company. He couldn't bear it.

Finally, he heard Connor at the door, saying, "I beg your pardon once again, Eva. Sometimes I can't believe my clumsiness. But you are so patient. Shall I see you next week? I shall do better then." He laughed and Adam groaned and ground his teeth together.

Adam stood, forehead against the door, steadying his heart rate and fighting to control the rage that filled his mind. He'd vowed never to lose his temper again but this was insufferable, like a knife twisting in his stomach. By the time he trusted himself to open the door, the parlour was empty and Eva was coming out of her room, tucking her neckerchief into her stays. Her apron was over her arm and she shook it out and tied it around her waist.

He stared at her; his eyes wide. She showed no shame at being seen dressing.

He finally found his voice. "I'd never have believed it of you!"

"Believed what...?" She frowned in confusion.

"I thought you had more self-respect! I thought... well, it doesn't matter what I thought but if that's how you earn your money, I don't want it. You owe me nothing. I don't want to be responsible for... for *this*!"

"For what? I don't understand! Please explain yourself!"

Adam's throat had closed. He was beyond speaking.

"Whatever you think, Adam, I intend to pay every penny I owe you. And how I do that, is no concern of yours. I won't apologise for helping people. I see nothing wrong in that!"

"Like that babbling fool?"

"If you mean Mr Connor, you're being insufferably offensive. He's a pleasant enough man. I help him and he appreciates it. I'm happy to make a difference to his life."

"A difference! How can you brazenly tell me that? And despite what you say, it does concern me! When you said you'd work, I thought you'd take in washing or sewing..."

"Why should I be paid very little for doing what many others can do, when I have other skills?"

"Skills!" He ran a hand distractedly through his hair and stared at her. "I'm not so sure I'd refer to what you offer as *skills*! Surely any woman can do that?"

Eva blinked rapidly and frowned. "What do you mean? Not all women are fortunate enough to be educated!"

"Educated? Well, that's a strange way to describe it!"

Eva stared at him and suddenly her eyebrows rose. She gasped. "Please tell me you understand people have been paying me for my reading and writing skills...?"

Adam stared at her. "Y...your reading and writing skills?"

She slowly shook her head. "What a nasty, suspicious man you are." Her eyes narrowed with anger and turning on her heel, she walked into her bedroom, slamming the door behind her.

Eva ignored the tap on her door which came several minutes later but

Adam continued to knock and when she finally opened it, his face was contrite.

"It appears once again I owe you my deepest apology. I don't know how to even begin to make up for my suspicions. But Bartholomew told me Mrs Roper used to run a bawdy house in London and I—"

"And you assumed she was running one here with me?"

"Well, when I saw you dressing—"

"I wasn't dressing! I'd merely changed my apron and skirt. Mr Connor knocked the ink over and it ran across the table and on to me. See!" she said, pointing at the dark stain on the table.

"I see now..."

"And you thought I'd... We'd... Here in this room?" She gestured towards the parlour, shaking her head in disbelief.

"I must admit, now, it seems unlikely but when I heard you—"

"You were eavesdropping?"

"I..."

"Enough!" How dare he judge her! Her pulse was racing and her heart thudding in her chest as fury raced through her veins. Fearing she might scream at him, she fought to keep her voice steady. "Since my father died, I've been tricked by a high-class bawd who intended to sell my virtue. I've been harassed by various members of the crew on board ship – one of whom took a bet he could take my virtue. And as you know, several of the farmhands at Prichard's farm attempted to persuade me too. But I have *never, ever* given myself to anyone! If you think earning money to pay you back is so important that I'd sell myself, then you don't know me at all!" Her voice grew shriller and louder. "But wait, I forget you *don't* know me at all! And certainly not well enough to judge me!"

Her chin trembled so much she couldn't carry on. But what else was there to say? In the silence, she suddenly realised how loudly she'd been shouting at him. Well, what did it matter? He already had such a poor opinion of her; it could hardly sink lower because she'd shrieked at him like a fishwife.

Colour had drained from his face but he merely stared at her silently.

She'd had enough of his reproach but as she tried to slam the door, Adam held his foot in the way.

"Please allow me to explain fully," Adam said, softly, "I didn't want to believe the worst in you, but when you wouldn't tell me what you did for your clients..."

"The reason I didn't tell you was because you made it clear that day we stayed in the George Inn you wanted nothing to do with me! So, how

I earn money is my business alone."

"I see, but I was afraid you were being taken advantage of and you were being hurt..."

Eva stared at him. "You were afraid... for me? I find it most strange you kept Kathleen's death from me to save me from pain and you fear for my welfare now. And yet, you've made it clear you have no regard for me at all!"

Adam squeezed his eyes shut tightly and shook his head as if not able to believe what he was about to say. "I can see how it appears I blow hot and cold but the truth is I've fought against this for as long as I've known you, Eva, but I can't deny it any longer. Hearing you with another man made me realise I love you. I didn't want to admit it because I'd told myself for so long I needed to be single–minded about going home. But every time I see you, I fall for you over again. And when I'm not with you, life's empty – and it'll be so, wherever I am."

He tried to open the door further but she blocked his efforts, her expression, one of shock and confusion.

"Eva? Please tell me you have feelings for me... You did once, I know you did."

She stared at him and slowly shook her head. Her voice was a whisper. "I'm sorry, Adam, I can't return your feelings." She pushed the door closed and locked it.

"Then, I'll leave you in peace." His voice was polite.

Minutes later, she heard his footsteps echo down the passage. The front door opened and closed.

Mrs Roper had been listening and as soon as Adam had gone she knocked on Eva's door.

"What happened? Where's your young man gone?"

Eva swallowed her tears and explained. Mrs Roper, hands on hips, stared at her in disbelief. "'E told you he loved you and you said you didn't want him? Have you taken leave of your senses?" She crossed her arms over her large bosom. "In my parlour, now!"

She led the way without looking back over her shoulder as if she knew Eva wouldn't dare disobey.

"Why on earth would you tell him that?" Mrs Roper slammed cups and saucers on the table. Eva winced at the sound of china clashing against china.

"It's obvious you belong together. It must've been determined at birth; look at your names, the Good Lord even decided you belong together!" Mrs Roper slammed the sugar bowl down on the table.

"I believe Adam's wife was Eve, not Eva."

"Fiddle-faddle!" Mrs Roper wagged her finger, "Adam and Eve, or Adam and Eva. It don't matter. You belong together. It's in the Bible. So?" she thumped the table with her fist, making the cups jump. "Why did you send him away?"

"E... everyone I've ever loved has been taken from me," Eva dabbed her eyes with her handkerchief, "my parents, my brother and sister, my friend... I've found it's easier not to love."

"Really?" Mrs Roper drummed her fingers on the table. If Eva had expected sympathy, it appeared she was going to be disappointed.

"Life's painful and you'd best get used to it, my girl. You can't exclude people from your life lest you lose them in the future. Enjoy their love while you can. You don't know how lucky you are to 'ave known love. Some of us ain't been so lucky. Some of us..." She tapped her chest with her finger, "were deserted at birth, grew up in the poorhouse and made their way in a world where people use you up until you're spent. Then they discard you." Her eyes had filled with tears but she was determined to continue. She swallowed and carried on, "Ain't no one ever told me they love me for being me. They just wanted me fer what I could do fer *them*." Her chin quivered and she was silent. The only sound in the room was the bubbling of the water in the kettle. Eva looked at the older woman who was staring into the distance, her face twisted in pain.

"I ... I'm so sorry." Eva reached out to place her hand over Mrs Roper's but before she could offer any comfort, the landlady had risen silently and gone to the spluttering kettle. She lifted it off the stove, then busied herself brewing the sweet-tea leaves. By the time she carried the tea to the table, she'd recovered her composure.

"Spare yer pity." Her voice was calm but flat. "I never 'ad a man what cared a jot about me... What I wouldn't give..." She poured the tea into the cups. "But you! You 'ad it right there in the palm of your hand..." She shook her head and clicked her tongue.

The fiery rage in Eva's blood had chilled. She'd been so certain she'd been right to try to protect herself but now, a cold, lonely future opened up in front of her.

They sipped tea in silence, then Eva rose to leave. "Thank you, Mrs Roper, I'm sorry your life turned out that way but I... I'll think about what you said."

During the next few days, Eva struggled to unravel her thoughts. How could it be wrong to try to avoid pain? The situation had seemed so simple before Mrs Roper had spoken her mind. You wouldn't touch a burning pot twice... although Eva could imagine Mrs Roper, with her down-to-earth sense, saying you'd never get to the soup unless you made some effort to grab the pan.

Adam's two rejections had been painful. It was true he'd explained why he'd pushed her away when he'd declared his love but still, what was the point? He'd soon be going home to Cornwall.

Anyway, what did it matter? She'd turned Adam down and now it was too late. Perhaps if he'd come back and begged her... But he hadn't and why should he? She'd rejected him. No, despite Mrs Roper's urging, it was too late for her and Adam. Biblical or not.

On Friday when Mrs Roper called for the rent, she told Eva she'd heard the governor had decided to grant early pardons to many of the convicts who'd shown themselves to be responsible and reliable.

"So, Adam might be gone soon?" Eva's stomach churned with disappointment and longing. Suddenly, the thought of never seeing him again was unbearable. Far from being the release she'd imagined it would be, his departure was too painful to contemplate.

"I can see you're having second thoughts about letting him go," Mrs Roper said.

Eva nodded. "It's too late now." Tears pricked her eyelids.

"Fiddle-faddle. 'Tisn't too late at all."

"What can I do?" Eva whispered.

"You know exactly what to do, my girl! Find him. And pray to God you're not too late."

Too late. Eva couldn't bear the thought. She'd go and see if the *May Queen* had returned to Sydney Cove and if it had, she'd find Adam. And say what? Words tripped over themselves as she tried to assemble her thoughts. Suppose she couldn't find him? A letter. That was the answer. She could put the chaos that swirled in her brain into some sort of order if she wrote down how she felt. And if she couldn't find him, she'd leave the letter at Shaw and Trevelyan's office.

When Mrs Roper had gone, Eva sat at the table and after wiping her palms on her apron, she picked up the pen. This had to be perfect. She had to find the right words. Dipping the pen in the ink, she wrote:

Dear Adam,

First, I would like to beg your pardon for telling you I had no feelings for you. It was merely wishful thinking. It would have made life easier for me, had I not fallen in love with you. But the truth is, I care about you deeply and I have done so, since those days when you came to my window at Pritchard's farm.

So, why did I tell you otherwise? Perhaps if I explain that everyone I have ever loved is taken away from me, I hope you will understand the only way I could protect myself, was to reject you. I have since had reason to reconsider and I would humbly beg your pardon and ask if you would give me a second chance. I understand you will be leaving for England soon and I cannot bear the thought of never seeing you again,

Your loving Eva.

She cringed every time she read it, but she risked running out of paper if she discarded any more letters.

Eva had never seen the *May Queen* before, although she knew where the sloop usually moored. As she reached the waterfront, she was relieved to see it rocking in the water, having feared Adam might still be away.

Now to find him and deliver her letter. He wasn't on board and she turned towards *Shaw and Trevelyan's* office opposite the boat when she saw Adam come out. Eva hadn't expected to find him so easily. Perhaps Mrs Roper was right about them belonging together. She cautioned herself against celebrating too soon – after all, he still had to agree to give her another chance. But as she hastened her step towards him, avoiding a man pushing a wheelbarrow loaded with boxes, Eva saw Adam offer his arm to a young woman who followed him out of the office.

In one hand, she held a yellow parasol which matched her exquisitely made frock and in the other, she held Adam's arm, looking up at him and laughing at something he'd said.

The couple walked towards the *May Queen* and Mr Shaw stood in the doorway of the office watching them with a satisfied smile. Adam helped the woman into the boat and her tinkling laugh rang out as her foot tangled in her skirt and she almost tripped. Adam caught her and she clung to him for longer than Eva thought was seemly. Mr Shaw waved from the doorway, turned and went back inside as if having given his blessing to his junior partner and the young woman being on the boat together. Adam had mentioned Bartholomew Shaw had one child – a daughter. Perhaps he too, had heard of the early pardons the governor had granted and wanted to push the couple together to keep Adam in Sydney and to consolidate the family business. But whoever the woman was, it was clear Eva could not now deliver the letter which declared her love for Adam. His interest lay elsewhere.

Biblical or not, this Adam and Eva would not become a couple.

Her heart felt like lead in her chest. Cold and dead. She turned and walked back to Mrs Roper's house where the landlady was waiting on the doorstep, hands on hips and head on one side. "Well?"

Eva slowly shook her head. Her eyes vacant. "I didn't speak to him.

He was with another woman."

Mrs Roper stamped her foot. "And?"

"It wasn't appropriate—"

"Appropriate? You can't afford to be *appropriate*!"

"But he was with someone else!"

"You don't want to let small details like that stand in your way!"

Mrs Roper stood in the doorway, arms crossed over her chest. She shook her head slowly and stepped to one side, allowing Eva to pass and to go to her rooms.

Mrs Roper was angry. There was no point relying on guardian angels. If you wanted something done, it was best to take matters into your own hands.

Literally.

As Eva had passed her in the doorway Mrs Roper had dipped into her pocket and removed the undelivered letter. Now as she slipped into the street tying the strings of her bonnet, she put her hand in *her* pocket and gave the letter a reassuring pat.

The sun beat down and she wiped a trickle of sweat from her cheek. It wasn't the sort of weather for speed, nevertheless, she quickened her pace to where she knew the *May Queen* was moored. When she arrived, Adam was on the deck with one of the boat hands and a woman was waiting on the shore, watching him – presumably the same woman Eva had seen.

Despite the shade afforded by the parasol, the woman was still in the full blaze of the sun and yet, she remained there, watching Adam and from time to time, calling out almost as if reminding him she was there because he was chatting to the other man and had indeed, seemed to have forgotten. Yes, it appeared the woman had feelings for Adam which were not reciprocated.

Perhaps it wasn't too late for Eva, after all. Adam couldn't be considering a match with this woman. Could he?

Adam and Eva. Yes, they would be together. Angels or no angels, Mrs Roper would make sure of it.

She marched to the *May Queen*. "Mr Trevelyan!" she waved her hand and ignored the woman's annoyed glances.

Adam leaned over the gunwale, his face registering concern. "Mrs Roper? Is aught amiss?"

"Mr Trevelyan, I have an important letter for you which needs your immediate attention."

Adam jumped on to the shore. "Is it Eva?" He frowned anxiously.

Mrs Roper allowed herself the glimmer of a smile at his apparent concern.

"Mayhaps," she said and turning her back towards the woman, she handed the letter over. "You may wish to read this in private."

"I beg your pardon, Miss Shaw," Adam said, turning to the woman, "but I'm afraid there are matters concerning my lodgings, which need my attention."

Miss Shaw simpered, and Mrs Roper saw the flash of annoyance. And now she recognised her as the young unmarried daughter of Bartholomew Shaw and if she was reading the situation correctly, the Shaw family would benefit greatly from a match between Adam and this snub-nosed, pouting woman.

"I trust I'll see you later, Mr Trevelyan," Miss Shaw said and walked back to her father's office.

Adam opened the letter and read it. When he'd finished he looked up at Mrs Roper in confusion. "If Eva means this, why didn't she bring the letter herself?"

"Because she saw you earlier with Miss Shaw and she assumed her letter wouldn't be welcome. If you need to know more, you must ask Eva yourself."

"I will. I'll go now."

Adam's eyes sparkled. He thanked her, put the letter in his pocket and strode towards Mr Shaw's office. Mrs Roper hurried home and let herself in quietly before Adam came to claim his Eva. A job well done and no angels had been required.

The heat had intensified and by the time Mrs Roper arrived home, she was drained. She splashed herself with water, poured herself a large glass of gin, then sat in her chair to recover. She was beginning to doze off when she heard Adam knock at the door. Eva let him in and there were footsteps down the passage. Mrs Roper allowed herself a satisfied smile and then slid back into her nap.

She awoke about ten minutes later. Adam was there all right. She could hear voices. That was a shame. She'd have hoped by now, they'd have discussed everything and were making up for lost time. But the conversation was becoming more heated. What was there to talk about?

Something smashed in Eva's room and Mrs Roper leapt to her feet. She would knock their heads together! But as she stepped into the passage, Eva's door opened and a man flew out backwards, slamming into the passage wall. He staggered to his feet and pushed past Mrs Roper and out of the front door.

CHAPTER THIRTEEN

Eva's rooms were oppressive. Earlier, there'd been a slight breeze but now, all was calm, as the sun scorched Sydney, blasting it with an intense brightness that made the eyes water.

Since she hadn't been expecting anyone, she'd assumed the knock on the front door was a visitor for Mrs Roper. To her dismay, it had been Mr Connor, who'd announced he'd arrived for his lesson. Eva had explained he was a day early but he'd begged her to put the lesson forward now he was there and although she'd been slightly alarmed because she could smell rum on his breath, he'd always behaved like a gentleman before.

She'd let him in, cleared the table and started the lesson but it soon became clear his mind was not on his letters and Eva had snatched her arm away when he'd started to stroke it. She'd leapt to her feet and suggested Mr Connor might like to leave as she'd remembered she had a prior arrangement. He hadn't been too drunk to realise he'd been impolite, and he'd apologised in a slurred voice but explained since she lived alone in the house of a known bawd, he'd thought she might be willing to earn a few more shillings. He'd tried to grab her but the drink had slowed his reactions and she'd easily evaded his grasping hands. Then, brandishing a saucepan, she'd told him to leave and not come back. A shove out of her door had finished the job and luckily, Mrs Roper had appeared and Mr Connor had decided it wise to depart.

Eva assured Mrs Roper she was fine but the incident with Mr Connor had shaken her and she was inexplicably close to tears.

That evening, she tried to read but couldn't concentrate, her mind drifting back to the woman in yellow with her arm through Adam's and the unwelcome attentions of Mr Connor.

It's hot and I'm tired.

She couldn't wait for the relative cool of nightfall and she promised herself she'd be better in the morning.

Later, when the sun was an orange ball low on the horizon and the heat had barely decreased, promising a sticky, uncomfortable night, Eva decided to go to bed. The storm which was threatening, still rumbled on the horizon but seemed in no hurry to pass overhead and deliver a downpour to cool the air.

Eva unpinned her hair and gratefully removed her clothes. She sponged her body with water and while still wet, put on her nightshift which clung to her body and cooled her slightly. She lay on the bed but, as tired as she was, sleep eluded her as she remembered Mr Connor's hands pawing at her arm as he pleaded with her that he was a good man and he would pay her and treat her well.

He'd believed he could take advantage of her because she carried out her lessons and lived alone. How could she ever gain people's respect?

It was so unfair. All she wanted was to live independently and to support herself but even on the far side of the world, social expectations were hampering a single woman's attempt to earn a living.

It was clear she wouldn't be able to conduct lessons for men nor read them their letters in her room unless she had a chaperone. Perhaps she could teach women? Were there enough women who wanted to learn to read and write? Should she get a large dog?

Despite the heat of the night and her pressing problems, she slid into a troubled sleep, dreaming of other oppressively hot nights spent in her tiny room in the Pritchard's farm with the hum of insects, the scrabbling of animals in the bush, and the ceaseless lapping of the river on the shoreline. Now, the sounds were mostly man-made; singing from the local inn accompanied by a lively fiddle or the yelling of two brawling men in the street. She had no wish to be back on the farm in Parramatta where life was much harder. But with longing, she dreamed of Adam waiting at a respectful distance from her window after having cleared his throat to warn her of his presence and then calling her name softly on the sultry night air.

Eva, Eva.

She reached out to him through the window but abruptly, he turned away from her, his attention now on the woman dressed in yellow who held on to his arm. He bent to kiss her and she lowered the parasol to hide their faces from Eva.

If only Eva hadn't sent Adam away. If only she'd given him the letter. If only...

Eva, Eva.

She sat up in bed, dreams and sleep receding. The sound was so convincing, it could almost be real. With a start, she realised someone really was calling her. Could that dreadful man Connor have come back? Well, she would show him! How dare he! She picked up the jug of water, intending to douse his ardour and if that didn't work, she'd smash the jug over his head.

She crept across the floor, jerked back the curtain and hurled the contents over the dark figure standing a short way from the window, then, held the jug aloft in case that didn't deter him.

The man gasped and spluttered. But it wasn't Mr Connor.

"Adam!" She gulped in horror.

In the moonlight, drops of water flew like diamonds from his hair as he shook his head.

"Adam! What are you doing here?"

"I wanted to discuss this." He held up a soggy piece of paper. "But I suspect the words have all disappeared after my soaking."

"Is it your pardon?" Her throat was so dry, she barely managed to form the words.

"Pardon? No. Not yet. Have you forgotten I still have quite some time to serve?"

"Mrs Roper hinted you might have a pardon," Eva said, "So?" She gestured to the dripping letter. "What's that?"

He held it out to her and as the moonlight fell on one small corner which had escaped the water, she gasped as she recognised her writing.

"Mrs Roper delivered it for you earlier today. I'd have come immediately but Bartholomew fell and knocked himself out. I stayed with him in hospital until he gained consciousness, then I came here."

"Mrs Roper? But I didn't give it to Mrs Roper..."

"So, you didn't..." His voice faltered, "you didn't mean what you wrote?"

"Yes, I did. But I didn't give it to her..." Suddenly, things became clear. "Oh! I see! She picked my pocket! And I expect she made up the story about the governor giving early pardons!"

"Why would she do that?"

"She believes we should be together. Because of our names. In fact, she was the one who told me to find you—"

"I see." Adam's tone was clipped. "So, what you're telling me is the landlady organised everything because *she* believes we should be together? I wouldn't have rushed away from Bartholomew's bedside if I'd known you were simply carrying out her wishes..."

"No! It isn't like that!" She put down the jug and held on to the window frame.

"Then what is it like?" His voice was hard.

Words tripped over themselves as she tried to explain her feelings. *Don't tell him, show him. Don't risk him walking away.*

Eva leaned through the window and seized Adam's jacket, then pulled him towards her. Wrapping her arms around his neck, she kissed him on his mouth – still wet from the water she'd thrown over him. She breathed in, taking in the faint smell of soap and the scent of Adam that had become so welcome all those months ago when he'd kissed her through a different window.

After a moment's shock, he took her face in his hands and looked deeply into her eyes. "Please, Eva," he whispered, "tell me you meant what you said in the letter...Tell me you meant that kiss..."

"I did! I do!" Laughter bubbled in her throat at the feelings of exhilaration which coursed through her. "I love you and I've always loved you."

He peeled her arms from his neck and stepped back.

"Adam?" Her voice trembled. Surely, he didn't intend to reject her again? She couldn't bear it.

But he was smiling. "I want to hear you say it again! You look like a beautiful portrait in a frame and the next time I sail, I want to remember you like a living painting, telling me you love me."

Eva's face fell. "When you sail?" she echoed sadly. Disappointment squeezed her heart. How stupid to have got carried away. Adam was already talking about leaving.

"On the *May Queen*. My next trip up the Parramatta... Did you think I meant when I go back to England?"

Eva nodded, the lump in her throat stopping her words.

"I won't remember you like this, in a picture frame when I go back to England because you'll be at my side... if you want to be, of course."

She could see them in her imagination. Almost smell the sea breeze and feel the spray on her face. But this time, they'd be free together. Free. Her hand flew to her chest as she remembered. "But you'll be free before me."

"I'll wait for you."

"Adam, this isn't what you want!"

"What I want, Eva – is you. I've thought it through and if you'll have me, we'll return to England together."

"But what about your family? You told me you need to provide for them."

"And so, I shall. I can send banker's drafts home to them."

"It was so important to you to go home before. I don't want you to resent me once you're free." Why was she trying to talk him out of it? This was what she longed for. But her heart couldn't bear to be broken again.

He stepped towards her and taking her hands. "It seems I was wrong about the urgency to go home. That thought kept me going when I first arrived here. And, yes, I want to support my family financially but I can do that from here. I also want to clear my name but there's no hurry... And if I'm honest, I wanted to prove to certain people I could be successful. But now, it's of no concern to me what people think. I intend to live my life for me, and for you, if you'll have me."

He raised her hands to his lips.

Eva threw her arms around his neck. "Yes, oh, yes!"

Raindrops began to drum on the dusty earth as the storm finally reached them.

"You must come in," she said and disentangling herself, she opened the door.

He hesitated. "Perhaps you'd like to cover yourself first? With you dressed like that, I can't be responsible for my actions."

She gasped with horror as she looked down at the damp nightshift that clung to the contours of her body. Her cheeks flamed as she wrapped her arms around herself trying to hide.

"Don't be embarrassed. I've never seen anything so beautiful." He stood back, waiting for her to close the door and find something to cover herself.

She knew he'd wait outside in the torrential rain until she was dressed, showing her the respect he'd always shown her. But hadn't they spent too much time apart and too much time being polite to each other?

She offered him her hand and when he took it, she drew him into the room, closed the door and put her arms around his neck.

"Is this truly what you want?" His voice was low and husky.

She nodded. "We've spent too much time trying to control our feelings to suit our lives. For once, shall we both act with our hearts and not our heads?"

His lips, wet from the rain, glided across hers, sending such exquisite feelings rippling through her body, she shivered with pleasure.

"Has no one ever warned you against wearing wet clothing? I hear it's bad for the health." He undid the ribbon around the neck of her nightshift and allowed the garment to slide over her body and fall to the floor. As he picked her up in his arms and carried her to her bedroom, her heart hammered wildly, matching the beating of his heart and the drumming of the torrential rain outside. Tonight, she decided, she wouldn't worry about the possibility of losing Adam in the future – she would simply revel in the here and now.

"Why is it unwholesome for me to have wet clothing and not you?" she whispered, nuzzling his ear.

"Trust me, my love, I will be remedying that as soon as I can."

After laying her on the bed he fumbled at his buttons, pulling his clothes off and dropping them on the floor.

"Wait!" she said, as he climbed onto the bed.

Adam froze.

"I'm going to light a candle. This shouldn't be something done in the dark. As if we're ashamed... I want to see you. And I want you to see me. I want to share everything."

He got up with her and standing behind her, he kissed her neck, then placing his hands on her shoulders, he lightly stroked them down her back, following the contours of her waist and hips as she fumbled with the tinderbox.

"If you carry on behaving like that, I won't be able to strike a light! My hands are trembling so!" He carried on kissing her neck until finally, she managed to strike the steel against the flint, and light the candle.

"You were no help at all!" she said, turning in his arms, so they were face to face, then moved as one to the bed.

The two entwined figures moved rhythmically together, as the flickering light of the candle cast a yellow glow across their bodies. Long before they'd finished exploring and caressing, the flame guttered and, with a curl of smoke, it went out, leaving them in the enveloping darkness.

Chapter Fourteen

Eva retied the red ribbon around the box and placed it in the chest.

Their chest.

Mr and Mrs Adam Trevelyan's chest.

She tucked the box into the corner under the lace handkerchief Adam had once given her. In an hour, Mr and Mrs Trevelyan – both now free people – would board the *Royal Seraph* and their chest would be conveyed to the cabin they'd occupy on the long voyage.

A shiver of excitement coursed through her at the thought they would be going... she hesitated when her mind supplied the word 'home'. Not 'home' but back to England. The sandstone house several doors along from Mrs Roper, which they'd bought when they married, was now 'home'.

Despite their initial desperation to escape the place to which they'd been exiled and to return to the land of their birth, they'd both become accustomed to this strange country. Wild weather, exotic wildlife and seemingly endless acres of untamed land. Adam had bought Mr Shaw out of the business and the *May Queen* had been joined by a similar boat they called, *Eden* – so named at Mrs Roper's suggestion that Adam and Eva needed some sort of Eden – even if it wasn't a garden.

"Well, glory be!" Mrs Roper said when she discovered Eva and Adam were finally together, "You've restored my faith in the angels."

"I think you had more of a hand in our union than any angel!" Eva smiled at her fondly.

"Fiddle-faddle." Mrs Roper waved her hand dismissively. "But I don't mind telling you, this ageing angel is hangin' up her halo. I need a rest. You two have been exhausting!"

Eva was relieved that shortly after she and Adam had moved out, Mrs Roper had found a new lodger, a widower, called Sam Winters who appeared to idolise her. He'd proposed many times over the following months but Mrs Roper was happy as things were.

"No need fer any o' that marrying nonsense," she'd told Eva repeatedly with a wink, "I like things as they are."

Eva wondered whether Mrs Roper's guardian angel was napping and needed a prompt but somehow, it didn't seem likely. Perhaps marriage didn't suit everyone like it did Eva and Adam.

She looked down at the small box tied with red ribbon and a lump came to her throat at Adam's thoughtfulness. When he'd told her about their passage on the *Royal Seraph*, he'd handed her the box which he'd been concealing behind his back.

"I'm not sure what sort of box it was you imagined," he said, "but I hope this will do."

She'd wondered if perhaps it was an item of jewellery but when she'd opened the box and read the papers inside, she was more touched than if he'd bought her gold or jewels.

Shortly after they'd finally found each other, Eva had told Adam about her last night in prison in England. She'd been so upset, she'd pretended to place her hopes of seeing Keziah and Henry again, inside an imaginary box, tying it with red ribbon and hiding it away at the back of her mind. At some unknown time in the future when there was a possibility she might find her brother and sister again, she would retrieve it.

Unknown to her, Adam had made enquiries of his own about Keziah and Henry. His cousin lived in London, working as a lawyer, and Adam had asked him to help. Papers had later arrived which Adam placed in the box and then tied with ribbon.

And now, she knew where Keziah and Henry were, or where they'd been when the letters left England.

And later, she and Adam would start a voyage which would carry them back to her brother and sister.

"Is the chest packed?" Adam crouched by her side and placed an arm around her shoulders. She nodded and leaned against him.

"Excited?" He kissed her temple.

She nodded again. She was so excited that for the last few mornings, she'd been sick – and she hadn't even boarded the ship yet. But she knew Adam would look after her.

Mrs Roper had read Eva's palm and pronounced her future would be filled with family. "More family than you'd imagined," she'd said, and Eva assumed she meant Adam's family. She wasn't sure whether to believe in the reading but she clung to the hope it was true.

"Ready?" Adam asked, raising her to her feet and kissing her.

"If I'm by your side, Adam, I'm ready for anything."

* * *

If you enjoyed this story, please consider leaving a review on Amazon mybook.to/TheDuchessOfSydney. For information about other books in this series, please go to https://dawnknox.com and sign up for the newsletter. Thank you.

About the Author

Dawn spent much of her childhood making up stories filled with romance, drama and excitement. She loved fairy tales, although if she cast herself as a character, she'd more likely have played the part of the Court Jester than the Princess. She didn't recognise it at the time, but she was searching for the emotional depth in the stories she read. It wasn't enough to be told the Prince loved the Princess, she wanted to know how he felt and to see him declare his love. She wanted to see the wedding. And so, she'd furnish her stories with those details.

Nowadays, she hopes to write books that will engage readers' passions. From poignant stories set during the First World War to the zany antics of the inhabitants of the fictitious town of Basilwade; and from historical romances, to the fantasy adventures of a group of anthropomorphic animals led by a chicken with delusions of grandeur, she explores the richness and depth of human emotion.

A book by Dawn will offer laughter or tears – or anything in between, but if she touches your soul, she'll consider her job well done.

You can follow her here on https://dawnknox.com
Amazon Author Central: mybook.to/DawnKnox
on Facebook: https://www.facebook.com/DawnKnoxWriter
on Twitter: https://twitter.com/SunriseCalls
on Instagram: https://www.instagram.com/sunrisecalls/
on YouTube: shorturl.at/luDNQ

THE DUTCHES OF SYDNEY

The Lady Amelia Saga – Book One

Betrayed by her family and convicted of a crime she did not commit, Georgiana is sent halfway around the world to the penal colony of Sydney, New South Wales. Aboard the transport ship, the Lady Amelia, Lieutenant Francis Brooks, the ship's agent becomes her protector, taking her as his "sea-wife" – not because he has any interest in her but because he has been tasked with the duty.

Despite their mutual distrust, the attraction between them grows. But life has not played fair with Georgiana. She is bound by family secrets and lies. Will she ever be free again – free to be herself and free to love?

Order from Amazon: mybook.to/TheDuchessOfSydney
Paperback: ISBN: 9798814373588
eBook: ASIN: B09Z8LN4G9

THE OTHER PLACE

The Lady Amelia Saga – Book Three

1790 – the year Keziah Bonner and her younger brother, Henry, exchange one nightmare for another. If only she'd listened to her elder sister, Eva, the Bonner children might well have remained together. But headstrong Keziah had ignored her sister's pleas. Eva had been transported to the far side of the world for a crime she hadn't committed andKeziah and Henry had been sent to a London workhouse. When the prospect of work and a home in the countryside is on offer, both Keziah and Henry leap at the chance. But they soon discover they've exchanged the hardship of the workhouse for worse conditions in the cotton mill.

The charismatic but irresponsible nephew of the mill owner shows his interest in Keziah. But Matthew Gregory's attempts to demonstrate his feelings – however well-intentioned – invariably results in trouble for Keziah. Is Matthew yet another of Keziah's poor choices or will he be a major triumph?

Order from Amazon:
Paperback: ISBN
eBook: ASIN

The Dolphin's Kiss

The Lady Amelia Saga – Book Four

Born 1790; in Sydney, New South Wales, to wealthy parents, Abigail Moran is attractive and intelligent, and other than a birthmark on her hand that her mother loathes, she has everything she could desire. Soon, she'll marry handsome, witty, Hugh Hanville. Abigail's life is perfect. Or is it?
A chance meeting with a shopgirl, Lottie Jackson, sets in motion a chain of events that finds Abigail in the remote reaches of the Hawkesbury River with sea captain, Christopher Randall. He has inadvertently stumbled across the secret that binds Abigail and Lottie. Will he be able to help Abigail come to terms with the secret or will Fate keep them apart?

Order from Amazon:
Paperback: ISBN
eBook: ASIN

The Great War

100 Stories of 100 Words Honouring Those Who Lived And Died 100 Years Ago

One hundred short stories of ordinary men and women caught up in the extraordinary events of the Great War – a time of bloodshed, horror and heartache. One hundred stories, each told in exactly one hundred words, written one hundred years after they might have taken place. Life between the years of 1914 and 1918 presented a challenge for those fighting on the Front, as well as for those who were left at home—regardless of where that home might have been. These stories are an attempt to glimpse into the world of everyday people who were dealing with tragedies and life-changing events on such a scale that it was unprecedented in human history. In many of the stories, there is no mention of nationality, in a deliberate attempt to blur the lines between winners and losers, and to focus on the shared tragedies. This is a tribute to those who endured the Great War and its legacy, as well as a wish that future generations will forge such strong links of friendship that mankind will never again embark on such a destructive journey and will commit to peace between all nations.

"This is a book which everyone should read – the pure emotion which is portrayed in each and every story brings the whole of their experiences – whether at the front or at home – incredibly to life. Some stories moved me to tears with their simplicity, faith and sheer human endeavour." (Amazon)

Order from Amazon: mybook.to/TheGreatWar100

Paperback: ISBN 978-1532961595
eBook: ASIN B01FFRN7FW
Hardcover: ISBN 979-8413029800

THE FUTURE BROKERS
Written as DN Knox with Colin Payn

It's 2050 and George Williams considers himself a lucky man. It's a year since he—like millions of others—was forced out of his job by Artificial Intelligence. And a year since his near-fatal accident. But now, George's prospects are on the way up. With a state-of-the-art prosthetic arm and his sight restored, he's head-hunted to join a secret Government department—George cannot believe his luck.

He is right not to believe it. George's attraction to his beautiful boss, Serena, falters when he discovers her role in his sudden good fortune, and her intention to exploit the newly-acquired abilities he'd feared were the start of a mental breakdown.

But, it turns out both George and Serena are being twitched by a greater puppet master and ultimately, they must decide whose side they're on—those who want to combat Climate-Armageddon or the powerful leaders of the human race.

Order from Amazon: mybook.to/TheFutureBrokers
Paperback: ISBN 979-8723077676
eBook: ASIN B08Z9QYH5F

Printed in Great Britain
by Amazon

81835744R00078